The Price
Of The
Mountain Lily

LIANA BROOKS

OTHER WORKS

ALL I WANT FOR CHRISTMAS

All I Want For Christmas Is A Werewolf
All I Want For Christmas Is A Reaper
All I Want For Christmas Is A Gargoyle

FLEET OF MALIK

Bodies In Motion
Change of Momentum

HEROES AND VILLAINS

Even Villains Fall In Love
Even Villains Go To The Movies
Even Villains Have Interns
Even Villains Play The Hero (omnibus)
The Polar Terror

TIME AND SHADOWS

The Day Before
Convergence Point
Decoherence

SHORTER WORKS

Fey Lights
If You Give A Skeleton A 3D Printer
Prime Sensations
The Price Of The Mountain Lily

COLLECTIONS

Darkness and Good
Escape: The Liana Brooks Sci Fi Collection
The Complete Inklet Collection

Find other works by the author at www.lianabrooks.com

THE PRICE
OF THE
MOUNTAIN LILY

LIANA BROOKS

AUSTRALIA

Trade Paperback ISBN: 978-1-922434-82-1
Hardcover ISBN: 978-1-922434-83-8
eBook ISBN: 9798223494157

www.inkprintpress.com

National Library of Australia Cataloguing-in-Publication Data
Brooks, Liana 1982—
The Price Of The Mountain Lily
92p.   cm.
ISBN: 978-1-922434-82-1
Inkprint Press, Canberra, Australia
1. Fiction—Romance—Science Fiction 2. Fiction—Romance—Clean & Wholesome

Summary: Zuli Yalsmon's family barely ranks as Regarded after the assault that exiled her sister, so for her wedding week, she must accept whomever deigns to appear...

First Edition: February 2024

Cover design © Inkprint Press.

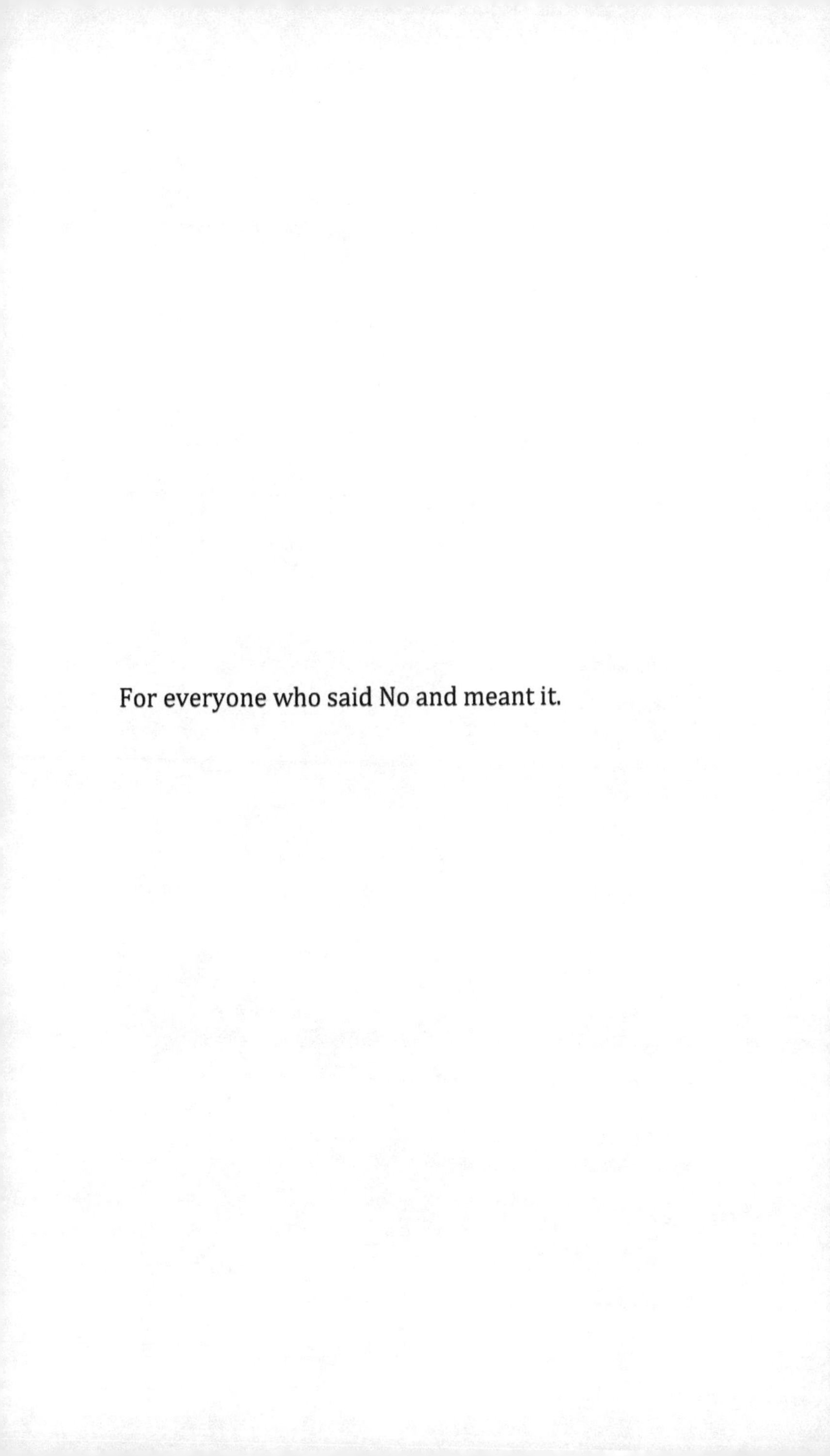

For everyone who said No and meant it.

THE PRICE OF THE MOUNTAIN LILY

Everything had a price.

Cool morning air, rich with the promise of a hot day, wrapped around Zuli with a lover's embrace as she contemplated her bleak future. An iridescent blue dragonfly with large golden eyes buzzed away, angry at her intrusion to the oft-forgotten balcony that overlooked the river.

Flowering vines twined around the gold-stone parapet made smooth by a century of worried Yalsmons straining to catch the first glimpse of an incoming ship down the raging waterway in the knife-cut canyon below.

The Worrier's Perch was what her mother called it. A contrast to the Warrior's See at the top of the household's central tower. Up on the See a person could survey the jagged mountains of the high desert for kilometers, see the signal lights coming off the watchtowers at the end of town, see the market flags in the center square, even see the spaceport in the valley to the south.

When she was young—when the Yalsmon family name still had power—she'd sat in the Warrior's See listening as her older sister memorized the meanings of each color and flag. They'd looked forward to the future like every other girl, eager to enter the markets with the hope of one day building enough capital to expand off-world to the stars.

It had been years since anyone in the family went up to the Warrior's See. On the rare occasions anyone did venture outside, it was to visit the silent isolation of the Worrier's Perch.

In the Worrier's Perch all one could see was the steep cliff face that dropped into the rolling, rushing white water of the Crescent Moon River as it cut its way from Piercing, where the first terraforming spikes had dropped, to Lansend on the plains, where the first spaceport had been built. It was a reminder of the past. Of the first, desperate women who fled distant wars and settled an uncharted solar system in the hope of finding peace.

Under the first hesitant touch of dawn the cliffs were a shimmering rose gold, old rock studded with shards of the broken sister-planet that Tanar had destroyed long before humanity had reached the solar system. Zuli and the planet had that in common: sisters lost to them for eternity.

A silver light flickered in the milky blue sky above, sparkling and falling and then racing across the mountaintops towards the port.

This is what Zuli had woken early to see. The poets said it was the tears of hope when the veil of night lifted. In the moments before true dawn, when the sky filled with a million silver stars sparkling like diamonds along the horizon, one could see beyond the limits of the world.

Zuli soaked in the sight of the glittering space stations, orbitals and ships, all named for explorers like she'd wanted to be in her youth, wondering if Adalet was up there. The older sister she might never see again.

Adalet the fiery. Adalet the tempest.

Adalet the banished.

Adalet that—like Tanar's twin planet—was destroyed and could never come home.

Soft footfalls covered by silk slippers warned Zuli to look away before her eyes filled with tears. She turned from the fading stars above to watch the windskippers darting from their nests on the cliff to catch the insects dancing over the froth of the river.

"Azuli?" Her mother's voice was soft as a lullaby. A gentle hand rested on her shoulder. "Why are you up so early, my flower?"

"Trouble adjusting to the time zones," Zuli lied. "I feel like I ought to be getting ready for class."

Her mother patted her shoulder, stroking the rippled embroidery patterns on Zuli's sleeve. "It is that way with new graduates. For twenty-five years we tell our daughters to hurry, to learn, to excel so they can do their merchant families proud. And then we call you back to work. To marry. To inherit. It is an odd thing, no? That there is no space between learning and doing? No moment to breathe, to rest, to appreciate all the fine work you've done?"

There was a quiet rebuke in her mother's words.

Zuli smiled as she turned to her mother. "I'm not asking to take time away from the family. It's just... odd, being my own boss."

"You're well-prepared." The light caught on the fading metallic thread in her mother's shawl and the silver in her midnight-black hair. Many years ago Azuri Yalsmon had been the most beautiful woman in the village of Samat. A brilliant statistician gifted with an understanding of the market's mercurial moods.

Even now, as the fortunes of the family faded like the gilt on their gowns, Azuri was respected and beautiful. Held back, the gossips said, by her risk-taking husband.

It would have been a sad end if theirs weren't a love match.

Squishing an insolent surge of regret, Zuli turned back to study the flowers, a deep purple bloom that fell into a yellow heart with a bright orange stamen hidden deep inside where only curious little girls and the pollinators ever bothered to look. The flowers had been Zuli's first lesson in life, and a good one, showing her that in everything there was some secret not visible at first glance.

"Your cousins should be arriving tomorrow," her mother said in the quiet voice of a mourner. "In three days it all begins."

The bridal announcement.

The bride's night, where she would stand before every suitor who would come, and choose her future husband.

The bride's dawning, when she and the man she chose announced their upcoming marriage to the world.

It was meant to be a joyous occasion. A grand tradition kept on because the people who grew Tanar from cold stone to rich planet were people who loved drama.

Pomp and circumstance.

If the Yalsmons had been a Grand-Tier family, with blue diamonds sewn to their cloaks and blue gold woven in their braids, this week would be joyous. Her cousins would be dressed in the finest couture. Household servants would be lavished with riches well beyond what they could have earned working for any other family. Zuli would be free to marry anyone, or no one at all.

But the Yalsmons had never been Grand-Tier, not even at the height of their power.

They'd never even been a High Family.

They were a Regarded Family, powerful in their own circle but without interstellar interests or control. Their wealth was sufficient for influence on the planet, but it wasn't exceptional.

That had been before her older sister had been banished. When Adalet had graduated early, there'd been a surge of interest. The High Families wanted new genetic material and Zuli's beautiful, intelligent, vivacious sister had had everyone's attention.

Those had been the good days.

Until Esko Ferith had taken an interest. Second son of a High-Tier merchant family, smiling snake, unworthy crocodile of a man.

"Zuli." Her mother tapped her tight shoulders. "It is no one's fault."

"She should have pushed him into the river and let him drown."

"Then there would have been a murder inquiry," her mother said calmly.

"He attacked her!" Brutally assaulted Adalet, and Ada had defended herself in turn. Before her sister was even safely home and the security officers could be called, House Ferith had released a statement saying Adalet had tried to seduce Esko.

As if a beautiful woman in her prime wanted a shriveled ballsack of a man ten years her senior.

House Ferith said it was for wealth, and Ferith would accept the proposal.

Keeping Ada safe and buying her freedom with a returned bride price had bankrupted the family. Zuli had gone from the best schools in the system to the best in the village. Her future fell from the promise of everything she wanted to the reality that the promise had always been a lie.

The great equality of the people—the assurance that everyone contributing to Tanar meant stability for all—was a sham.

Tanar's culture was another caste system hidden under layers of platitudes and oppression. Looking down from a high perch, it was as silky smooth as the white river. It was only when you fell that you saw the waters were blue and the white was the froth reaching out to drown you in the chaotic misery of poverty.

"I'm going to run into the city," Zuli said. "There's a few things I left at my friend's house at the graduation party. And I need to buy bridal presents for the cousins." The traditional gifts of new clothes and jewels would have to wait. Her budget was small and her cousins even poorer than her. They'd understand.

Her mother sighed and looked out across the sun-dappled cliffs. "Don't be gone too long. I've already lost one daughter."

"I'll be safe," Zuli promised. "My bride price is practically set in stone. Jonthir has three small rubies to offer me."

"A pretty ring," her mother said softly, not looking away. "That used to be all the bride price was. A pretty ring and a promise of fidelity. It wasn't always business contracts and auctions."

It was hard to smile, but Zuli managed. "Sometimes there was love."

"More times than not, back when the forests were still young. When I was little and the mountains were bare. But, time passes and cultures change. We keep pushing for isolation, cutting off access to the spaceports, choking the markets." She sighed. "One day we're all going to die. I hope to close my eyes forever before the morning stars fall."

"All right, time for breakfast." Zuli steered her mother back towards the main house. "When you start quoting poetry it means you're hungry and if I don't feed you, you'll start yelling."

"Feed me?" her mother demanded as they crossed a neglected courtyard with tangled, dying vines and an algae-choked fountain. "I am not in my dotery! I can feed myself. Ungrateful child."

Wide wooden doors opened to a comfortable home with smooth brown-tiled floors flecked with gold, white-washed stone walls hung with art collected from hundreds of planets, and gemstone mosaics built into the doorframes.

Not rare gems, simple emeralds and topazes. The odd amethyst or sapphire. All swept up as debris after the first, violent moments of terraforming. Her ancestors had thrown most of them in the river, but a few had turned them into art. And, as mud and time buried the river gems, the remaining ones became more valuable.

Three small rubies was an insult.

Jonthir was buying her love for river rocks.

No, he was buying her future with river rocks. Her love she'd already given away freely to a man she was going to town to say goodbye to.

THERE WAS A KNOCK AT THE OFFICE DOOR. KYVAAN LOOKED up, first out the window at the sprawling, domed city of Mieka with the sea of silver light and the black-opal sky the tourist brochures loved to brag about, then to the interior wall and the office, which should have been empty.

"Come in." He shifted in his chair, stretching his neck and picking up the palm-sized displacer weapon from his pocket.

"Sorry to disturb your reading." His personal secretary walked in, a young man with a halo of brown curls and pastel orange eyes.

"Why didn't you go home on schedule?"

"I did." His secretary rolled his eyes at the obvious. "I met friends at the new restaurant in the third ward."

Kyvaan waited blank faced for more information.

His secretary stared back. "You were tracking that

there was a new restaurant in third ward? The one whose import license was in the news?"

Kyvaan narrowed his eyes. "When was this?"

"Ah..." His Miekan secretary did some mental calculations and then nodded in understanding. "You were off planet at the time. And it didn't seem important."

"But you came in late after work to tell me because...?"

He held out a hanfon. "You had me flag all of the trades attached to the land sales on the planet Nykiinos."

"The one above the gas giant neighbor everyone's preparing to mine? Yes." He'd only picked up forty-nine percent of the planet in the land auction, a failure that still grated on his nerves.

"Yes," his secretary said. "The terraforming team will be completing inspections and certifications this week. But Dala just sold."

Kyvaan stood up, dropping his displacer back in his pocket. "Dala Limited? Sold?"

Dala, the most vexatious and intriguing woman he'd ever met. With hair black as a starless night and lips set in a permanent smirk. The first night they'd met he'd been enchanted by her wit and by her lily-and-cardamom perfume. She spoke Trade3 with a slight Oleirian accent, but the mention of his homeworld of Tanar had turned her soft smile sharp.

They moved in the same circles, frequently bidding on the same investments. Sometimes he won. Sometimes she won. But always they danced around one another, never quite seeming to finding a place to meet.

"Dala doesn't sell," Kyvaan said. "I offered her triple what she paid for the fifty-one percent of the planet she bought." He had plans for a trade depot there. It was going to be a very wealthy system in the next decade.

His secretary flipped to the relevant screen. "Sold to a small trade union outside the Tanar System, who traded it for gems that were sold. The money was spent on a number of luxury items and gifted."

"To who?" Kyvaan scrolled down through the layers of trade and treachery. "Little Sister Holdings? Is that a translation error?" Interstellar trade had four major languages, all of which he knew, but he had never heard of Little Sister Holdings in any of them.

"It's an unknown company, three years old. They've made no major trades or purchases. They weren't flagged by any of our people, but I looked, because I was curious, and they seem to have acquired majority shares in a number of companies recently."

A pattern emerged amid the murk.

"Dala is selling to herself?" That had to be it. Over the past four years he'd studied Dala's trading habits. Spent countless hours pouring over the companies she purchased, how she changed them, as he tried to learn everything about his enigmatic, captivating rival.

"She's not listed on Little Sister Holdings," his secretary answered.

"Is it—" He stopped as the answer appeared on screen. "Hmm. Strange."

"Boss?" The secretary peered at the screen, trying to identify the problem.

"Dala's business movements feel Tanar-trained to me." Ruthless, focused, and done with an eye for the longevity of the benefit. Dala didn't look to make short term profits as a rule. She nurtured her purchases, set up unions, invested in making her companies safe and profitable for generations. And she'd grown her wealth exponentially doing it.

"But Little Sister Holdings isn't from Tanar. None of these are."

"No, that's what I find puzzling." Kyvaan kept looking. "Where did the gifts go?"

"Ah," the secretary took his hanfon back and searched his database. "Here, gifts were sent for the opening of a new trade depot on the moon of Welsol near the CrossFive trade route."

The names tickled an old memory. "Who were the investors?"

"Nunsan Investments, Mountain Lily Trade, River Peak Trade, and Oldfall Investments."

"Snow Mountain, Mountain Lily, River Peak, and Oldfall?"

"Nunsan, no translation. But, otherwise, yes." His secretary frowned with worry. "Is this a problem?"

Kyvaan shook his head. "Snow, Lily, River, and Oldfall are all mountains on Tanar Prime. Sites of upwelling and major mineral deposits with major cities. None had off-world trade centers before."

"So this is..." The secretary, Miekan born and raised, didn't know the politics of Tanar well enough to understand the implications.

"It's a new avenue of direct trade from an area rich with gems to the gem-buying worlds outside the Tanar system."

"Why not sell the gems on the planet?"

"Because diamonds the size of your head get pulled out of the river by children. They have no value on the planet. Export is controlled by edict of the ruling council and very few permits are allowed."

"So, Dala Limited is moving into gem sales?"

"Possibly, but more importantly, I'm going to Tanar."

"Why?"

"I need to talk to my grandmother." To find a Tanar-trained merchant and win her approval, he needed the best merchant on Tanar.

THE AIR RIDER WAS AN INDULGENT AND EXPENSIVE PIECE OF transport equipment. Especially the single-seater Zuli picked out of her parent's garage. It was older, with a tourmaline-blue bed and a clear half-globe top, looking a little like a magic carpet out of a children's storybook, if magic carpets shone like tear drops of the goddess against the pale blue sky or flew in excess of fifty kilometers a minute.

Inside the air rider, Zuli listened to the newest music from the central worlds—a new import, not actually new music. It was probably already several years old by the time it trickled to the Tanar System, and the vetting process for the music was over nineteen months, but it was new to her. She liked to imagine Adalet listening to the same music far away amid the stars.

She imagined her sister happy. Thriving. A cheerful smile on her lips. Her thick brown hair grown long again, rolling in waves down her back and catching the sunshine on some planet far away.

Catching the moonlight as her lover beckoned her closer.

Zuli closed her eyes as the air rider fell down to the city, her dream almost a prayer for her sister. One of them had to be happy. One of them deserved that much from the universe.

It wasn't like Jonthir was going to make any effort to please her. She was walking into a loveless marriage because her cousins needed the social ties the marriage would bring.

Jonthir's family was Regarded.

They weren't as skilled at business as the Yalsmons, but with her guidance they could prosper. She'd be able to ensure her parents were cared for as they aged. That the people who worked for her family were given generous retirement sums and enough to see their children go to better schools, reach new heights.

Her cousins would have better marriage offers because they would bring connections to Jonthir's import business.

All she had to do was suffer through actually being with him for the rest of her life.

The music shut off as the air rider landed outside the university grounds. The parking lot sparkled, still filled with air riders of every color. It was bridal season and most of the students would go home at some point, but she wasn't the only one putting it off to the very last minute.

As Zuli climbed out, she looked around for the plain, silver carriage and gray-topped air rider that belonged to Kamal.

It wasn't anywhere to be seen.

Sorrow struck like a rock ripping the hull of a river boat, quick and painful.

It was all becoming too real.

In school it had been so easy to pretend that this week would never come. That she and Kamal could have a lifetime together.

But here she was, alone in a field of gems, tears in her eyes.

"Really?" she asked herself and the world in general. "Really? You want to cry over a man whose full name you don't know? This is stupid."

Kamal of the Plains.

It was the kind of name you gave people when you didn't want to share your household affiliation. Sometimes the poorer folk did it, but usually it was something reserved for the wealthy. The High houses and the Grand ones.

She had introduced herself as Azuli of the White River just to tease him at that first party. It had been fun to think he was trying to puzzle out what important daughter she was, but then they'd danced in a garden filled with soft blue lights, and she'd never wanted to leave his arms.

With a sniff, she brushed away a rogue tear and marched back toward the main university campus. It was built much like her home, with a rounded outer wall filled surrounding elegantly appointed courtyards, winding stairs and halls, every window offering a view of some well-tended garden.

The stone here was a soft, pearly gray accented by mother-of-pearl and gray diamonds from the foot of the volcanoes near Piercing. Instead of art, great quotes were carved into the stone walls and wrapped with gold or accented by river gems.

A lime-scented breeze blew off the low desert, caught the sparkling mist off the courtyard fountains, and flew into the halls cooler and fresher than before.

Zuli followed a familiar route to the outer gardens at the school's front gate, where the din of the city could almost be heard over the splash of the great fountain and the warbling of the songbirds, everything as picturesque as the first day when her worried parents had dropped her here, swallowing their fears of losing another daughter to the city.

Daylight washed out the beauty of the outer garden.

It looked plain—no—flat with the sun overhead. There were no shadows to give it depth. No nuance of moonlight letting her see the blue and purple veins running through the dark green leaves of the vines.

The fragrant white jasmine flowers were closed against the heat of the day.

Still, she stopped, soaking it in one last time.

She'd first seen Kamal here, before the welcoming ceremonies, a glance across a busy garden on the first day of school. The flash of white teeth against a dark brown face as he grinned. The answering smile in his eyes when he looked at her. The lush, dark hair she wanted to run her hands through...

If she'd known how wonderful he was then, she would have waded through the fountain to meet him.

Although that might have made the wrong first impression.

The memory faded as reality reasserted itself.

Presents for the cousins. She needed to get her hand-com from the repair shop and then figure out what she could buy for the family with less than two hundred lyra.

She took the northernmost bridge away from the school and the wealthy end of town, crossing into a hilly neighborhood with small, rounded houses dug into the ground and shaded by citrus trees. It was quiet this early in the day. By noon it would be silent; even the birds and insects would go to ground. So would she, as soon as she reached the entrance to the shops near the local Warrior's See.

The sign beside the tower read FOR ABIGAIL.

Another daughter like Ada who never came home.

Stairs wound up the tower like a strangler fig, and down into the ground, widening as if to invite the heat-tortured souls standing under the sun to retreat into the welcome oasis of shadows. Further south in the city, the entrances to the underground were wider. Expensive homes had tunnels running from doorstep to shops so the wealthier citizens didn't have to risk the heat above ground.

Or, at least, not in the daylight.

Zuli found she didn't mind the dusty stairs, the air of neglect and regret. Empty shops and cracked paint suited her mood.

A bell jangled wearily as she opened the door to Hillview Repair Shop. Behind the counter an equally tired woman with her hair covered by a grass-green kerchief looked up. "Aye?"

"Zuli Yalsmon. I've come to pay for the repairs to my handcom." She shivered a little in the cold air meant to protect the precious electronics.

The tired woman sighed. "Right. The *hanfon*." She used the interstellar term for the com. "What did you do to it, daughter? I am a mother who sees many unruly children, but this?" She pulled the handcom out with the cracked, cherry-red case and a gray screen that had turned green. "How did you do this?"

"Would you believe I left it on the windowsill and it overheated?" Zuli asked.

"I'd believe this thing is older than my honored grandmother and needs to be replaced," the shopkeeper said. "It's trash. Fit only to be melted down and recycled." She dropped the handcom into a recycling bin with an air of finality.

Zuli's jaw dropped. "But... I... I need that! I have to access everything! My sister's contact is on there. My pictures." The only pictures of either Adalet or Kamal. "How... I... but..."

The shopkeep held up a slim data chip between two thick fingers. "The casing is gone, daughter. But the soul lives on."

"I can't afford a new casing!" Even the cheap ones cost seventy lyra and would eat away too much of her budget.

"Do I look like I was born under the last new moon?" the woman asked. "Of course I know a daughter carrying a phone like this can't afford another one. Especially when her husband comes in asking if I've seen a cracked cherry-red case."

"Husband?" Zuli's mind screeched to a halt. "What husband?" Jonthir would use this to lower his bid price. She'd be a bride with no price.

An embarrassment.

Her soul shriveled, taking away her will to live. Who ever heard of a woman marrying a man because he replaced her phone?

The shopkeeper raised bushy eyebrows. "A tall man, thick, dark hair. Handsome smile. Likes to talk? Said he was from the plains?"

"Oh. Him." She could breathe again. *Kamal.* "He's not my husband."

"Why not?"

"Ah, that's complicated." Technically there was no law against such a marriage, but it was taboo. Families from the Grand-Tier didn't marry down. They married out, choosing daughters of far-flung star systems to become their brides.

"He left lyra for you to pick a new body for your hanfon's soul. Do you want the lyra or the chip, daughter?"

"The new handcom. Hanfon. Please."

The shopkeep nodded and opened her display case. Gem tones were always in season, but there were more shell pink cases right now. Pink was a lucky color in the plains. Up in the mountains, pink skies meant windstorms coming through. Most of the cases were gaudy, fit for young girls and children.

Or old grandmothers who wanted to reclaim some lost time of their youth and play puzzles all day.

"Not enough for a business woman?" the shopkeep asked. "You have family colors?"

"Coppers and blue. Touches of gold and river brown. Tiger's eye and tourmaline." Zuli glanced at her. "I'm from the mountains."

"They raise strong daughters in the thin air," the woman said. "One of my sons is hoping to marry a mountain woman." There was a curl of a question in the woman's voice.

Zuli pulled herself away from the counter. "Has he picked a good gift for the bridal evening?"

"It's hard to say. Her family is Good, but not Regarded. Very small and young. Her parents work for a better house."

A daughter of servants then. "She's gone to school?"

"Yes, we met her when she was doing a survey for one of her classes. She had some interest in the manufacture of hanfons, wanted to see if they could be made here. Had questions about import."

Zuli nodded in understanding. "Your son will offer part of the business to her?"

"Part," the older woman agreed. "I have three sons to marry off. So a third of the business, a new air rider for her and her parents, and gems. But it is hard to know what gems and sparkles a woman like her would value." Again, it was a question disguised as a statement.

"Strong stones and carvings are always valued. Her family won't have much art if they are poorer. Offering her a pick of the art for the new home and the chance to gift her parents art on her first anniversary would be good. Imports are always luxury items and servants can't afford them."

"Who can these days?"

"So true." Her family hadn't bought anything new since before Adalet was banished. A problem she tried hard not to think about with her own bridal night fast approaching and her family's servants and kin expecting gifts of their own. "I wish your family a happy match."

The shopkeep's face wrinkled in a warm smile. "Such a good daughter. You have a business mind. Here. Let me show you something special." She reached behind her into a drawer and pulled out a small handcom so smooth it looked like liquid copper. She turned it over to reveal a delicate image of vines and flowers picked out in tiny blue gems.

Zuli's breath caught at the beauty. "Oh. That is...." *Perfect. Gorgeous. Fantastic.* "...Well out of my price range."

"Really?" The shopkeep seemed amused. "Your young husband seemed to think otherwise. He told me to hold it for you."

Her heart broke. The handcom was worth more than she'd ever earn as a bride. It would be the single most expensive thing in her house when she married.

It would also be the final gift from Kamal.

"Take it," the woman said.

"Thank you." Zuli waited for her to slide the chip in and hand over the powered handcom.

Kamal's face smiled up at her, framed by moon-white flowers.

"Have a happy bridal week," the old woman said as Zuli walked out.

"Thank you. Good luck with your son's proposal."

Outside she found a quiet corner between a closed shoe store and an empty garden to check her messages. There were updates from her cousins. A few rather cutting remarks from Jonthir's younger sister on a public forum. Several waiting messages from Kamal and one from someone calling from Dala Limited.

Curious, she tapped the button and opened the message. An almost-familiar woman looked at her with bright black eyes and thick brown hair wet from rain.

Adalet.

"Hello, baby sister! I heard that your bridal week was forthcoming and so I have begged and pleaded with the magistrates for permission to come send you off, barefoot and humble as I should."

Zuli shook her head wordlessly.

"I know you don't care," Adalet's recording said cheerfully. "But people will bring it up and I want everything to be just right for your wedding. I'm going to be there for you. To wish you joy. To see that all the traditions and customs are observed. To bring gifts!"

She held up a small, tattered brown bag.

Zuli could almost make out where the mountain lilies had once been embroidered in blue thread all those years ago.

It had been a clumsy gift for a beloved older sister. The threads had knotted and the bag was too small for much of anything. But Adalet had treasured it. Carried it with her everywhere as if it were the most expensive bag. Worn it at her hip in college. Folded a curl of her hair in it after it was shorn and taken it with her into banishment.

"Meet me, um," Adalet looked away from the messaging terminal, "three days after graduation? Yes, that looks right. Three days after. I should get there the day before the cousins do. Pick me up at the port. Yes? Yes! I'll see you then, my little gem."

Adalet blew a kiss as Zuli scrambled to understand.

Three days after.

A day before…

Adalet was at the spaceport today! Probably even now! She would come in on the dawn flight from the orbitals!

Holy mothers of flight!

Zuli had to get to the spaceport.

The study door slammed open loud enough to send the flock of pink parrots cooling themselves under the leaves of the Alocasia plants screaming into the fountain. Which lead to more screaming.

"What?" Kyvaan glared up from his notes, fully expecting to see some highborn son running amok and hoping to play in the fountain that splashed the outer patio and cooled the room.

His cousin, fully grown and freshly graduated from the local university, smiled back at him. The plain white tunic was casual wear at home, meaning his cousin was slumming it at the ancestral home as well.

Kyvaan rolled his eyes. "Go pester someone else."

"Why? What are you doing?"

"Torturing myself."

"Oh?" The door closed quietly as his cousin crossed the room to peer over his shoulder at the computer screen.

Curse his quick tongue. Of course his cousin would take that as an invitation.

"What's this? A buy out?" He stabbed at the screen. "Land measurements? Resource surveys? Are you buying a planet?"

"Bought," Kyvaan said through gritted teeth. "Or, partially bought. Nykiinos, on the outer shell of the Heflelin System. The moon is uninhabitable and a poor candidate for terraforming, but the planet is a small M-class one, breathable atmosphere, partially terraformed and habitable already. It comes with mining rights to the neighboring gas giant."

His cousin's eyebrows went up in an approving expression. "Heflelin is an easy stretch from the Tanar System. The mining rights will give us more fuel. Nice."

"Right. A good place for trade. A sterile moon for biological experimentation. Grandmother had me look into it and I acquired it with the plan of leasing it to various trade families."

"And? What happened?" His cousin sat on the edge of a desk. "Did unplanned seismic activity destroy your new toy? Volcano? Invasion of a crime syndicate?"

"No." This was exactly why he'd packed up and left the planet seven years ago. Family were too nosey. "I managed to get half the planet in the bidding war. The other half was scooped up by my darling nemesis, she of the lethal negotiating tactics, and now she's given it away."

Dala. If he breathed too deep he swore he could smell her lily-and-cardamom perfume. The scent that haunted so many auctions and all of his dreams.

"Given it away?" His cousin smelled blood in the water too.

"Sold it, at any rate. For a ridiculously low price. And not to me. I told her I'd pay her triple what she'd bought it for. She said sale was off the table. But, she's liquidating so many of her companies. Selling them. Cashing out. It makes no sense."

"Maybe she found something better to do with her life."

Kyvaan shook his head. "No, you don't know this woman. *I* barely know this woman. She came out of nowhere a few years ago and cut through the near systems like a shark. Snapped up little investment companies. Bought out rivals. I swear she's Tanar born. Uses our tactics, at any rate."

"Is that why you finally came home? To see if she was here?"

"No!" Not publicly. Mothers and grandmothers forfend. If anyone suspected he was considering taking a wife he'd not escape the gravity well. "I came to do a few in-person deals that were too delicate for delayed coms. I'm here for a week and then I'm leaving."

"Mmm. Does grandmother know that?"

"Of course."

"Well, then, maybe that's why she wants to see you."

Kyvaan stopped scrolling and blinked. "Surely you mean *us*."

"Nope." His cousin shrugged and meandered towards the patio, doing an excellent impression of a foppish heir with fewer brain cells than shoes on his feet. "She asked for you specifically."

"When was graduation?"

"Last week."

"It's bridal season?"

His cousin nodded in consoling agreement as he picked a berry up from the small tray a servant had brought in and tossed it to the birds. "Worst time to come home. Like you said, some negotiations don't work over delayed coms."

"I'm not here to get married!"

"Have fun explaining that to grandmama. You should get going."

Kyvaan locked his computer before he stood. "Yes, but not alone."

"What!" His cousin looked horrified. "Why would you drag me into this?"

"Because, I'm going to ask you a favor later today." He caught his cousin's sleeve as he passed and dragged him towards the hall.

"If I'm doing you a favor why am I being dragged to see grandmother? This doesn't feel like a way to build good will!"

"The only two reasons grandmother could possibly want to see me are to discuss new trade deals or a marriage. For one, you'd profit. For the other, it would be your marriage anyway. I'm making sure you don't miss any opportunities and that you aren't thrown unwilling into a marriage."

"This doesn't benefit me and you know it!" His cousin shook him off but fell into step anyway. "I have a woman picked out. I have the bids set aside for the Bridal Night."

"Really? The elusive woman you've never brought home?"

"She's shy!"

"The one who hasn't given you her name?"

"She will."

"Has she even told you where she lives?"

"White River?"

"Where is that?"

"The White River rages between the storm and the sea, racing the tide, touched by the goddess—"

"Poetry is not a mailing address!"

His cousin's hanfon chimed.

Stopping in the middle of the hall, his cousin checked the notification and smiled. "I should probably go."

"Why?"

"I'm about to hear good news." His cousin was already heading for the outer doors.

"About what?"

"The white river!"

THERE WAS NO WAY TO GET A PERMIT FOR ZULI'S FLYER THE day she needed to arrive at the spaceport. Not on such short notice. She'd need to park on the far edge of the city and have Ada walk across the burning rocks of the desert plains.

Requiring Ada to go barefoot and wear unadorned clothing was the worst punishment. In banishment Ada had complete control of her life, but no family. At home, she could have her family, but no other marker of favor, wealth, or power. Not until after Zuli's wedding.

Tapping her handcom on her thigh, Zuli let herself panic for forty-three seconds before she took a deep breath and dialed Kamal's number from memory.

"Hello." His voice was rich and silky, like a dark chocolate mousse. "How is the most beautiful woman in the world today?"

"My mother is doing well," Zuli said with a smile. "How are you?"

"Better, now that I've heard from you," Kamal said, and she could hear the cat-with-the-cream grin in his voice. "Is this about the date of your bridal night?"

The family's assessment was coming up in four days, and once the summary of the Yalsmon's wealth was public knowledge, Kamal would know why she evaded that question. For now she dodged with a playful laugh. "No, that's not set yet. We were waiting for some news about when family was arriving. But I didn't have my handcom and now my sister is arriving at the spaceport and I don't have a pass to go pick her up. Do you know anyone who can get in?"

"My cousin's flyer has the necessary passes," Kamal said.

"Do you think you could persuade your cousin to bring their flyer and come pick me up?"

"No."

Panic washed over her.

"But I can convince my cousin to lend me his flyer and come pick you up myself."

I love you. The words could never cross her lips. It would break her to hear Kamal loved her and then go to Jonthir on her wedding night. She was too poor to earn a better husband. Too poor for love to win.

Her family needed a secure, lucrative match. Kamal's family would want the same for him.

"Where are you?" Kamal asked.

"Near the Hillside See. I just picked up my handcom."

"And?" There was a nervous note in Kamal's voice.

"I love it," Zuli said. "It's the most beautiful handcom I've ever seen."

Kamal chuckled. "Did you like the colors I picked?"

"Yes. Very much." Her House colors. "It was a good guess."

"The colors of the mountain lily are copper and blue. The golden mountains and the sky's own hue." The poem was old, from the time of the first cities, a lament for a lost love and the price of progress demanding the blood of the workers.

Her heart broke. He knew. Somehow, he knew. "You're the most wonderful man. Have I told you that?"

"Almost enough times to make me believe it," Kamal said. "I'll be outside the See in five minutes. Do you want me to come in and meet you?"

"No, I'll be waiting." Always waiting. For him and for the life they might have had if Esko Ferith hadn't tried to steal Ada's future.

Zuli held Kamal's hand as he piloted the small ground flyer across the dust roads to the spaceport outside of town. "It's quiet today." She breathed in the scent of his cologne, trying to press every detail into her memory so she'd never forget.

"It's always quiet after graduation." He squeezed her hand and brought it up for a kiss. "Everyone's gone off to see relatives and attend bridal parties."

She looked resolutely out the window at the dry plain. "Very subtle." Sighing, she tried to smile. If nothing else, she could make sure their last moments together were happy. "What have you been doing since graduation?"

"The usual. I visited my parents' memorial. My aunties fussed over my rank as the highest scoring male student on the exams. My grandmother keeps inviting me to tea with 'old friends' who have granddaughters." He glanced at her, dark eyes full of hope. "She wants me to get married."

"Of course. That's what all matriarchs want. Sons have too little control of their genes to maintain a bloodline. They can give away pieces of themselves to every woman they meet, if they wished. A woman only receives and grows. Only a daughter's blood is proof the bloodline is maintained, protected, and not mixed without being recorded." That line of thought was enough to draw her eyes up into the dark azure sky looking for signs of the outer stations. "If we had a little more genetic diversity on the planet we wouldn't need to worry quite so much about maintaining records of blood lines."

"You know people wouldn't suddenly value sons as much as daughters just because of open trade. There's traditions."

"They used to be simpler," Zuli said, remembering what her mother had said.

"That's what everyone says." Kamal drove past the port's main gate without pausing.

A purple light on the front window of the transport blinked, but that was all.

"I must thank your cousin for the use of her flyer. She must travel frequently to be allowed to come and go as she pleases." Only a Grand-Tier family had extensive inter-stellar interests. A High-Tier family might have a few, but not enough to go to the port regularly.

Not for the first time, Zuli considered the possibility that Kamal's insistence on using 'of the Plains' implied wealth. If his cousin wasn't running errands for a Grand house, then she was from a Grand house, and even if Kamal's mother hadn't married into that tier she would want her son to marry up as her sister's had. A marriage to Zuli would be impossible. The difference between them was too wide an abyss for love to cross alone.

"My cousin is a he," Kamal said. "Kyvaan handles what remains of his mother's businesses, and she worked for the High Matriarch and the Planetary Counsel."

Zuli grew a little dizzy at the thought. The High Matriarch was the prime negotiator for the people. The most powerful woman on the planet. The first line of defense between the people of Tanar and the greedy nations all around. The most astute and cunning of women.

When Ada had been a student, the High Matriarch had still taken in the occasional protege, a daughter of a lesser House who showed promise and who benefited from the Matriarch's tutelage. Ada had once hinted she even had seen the High Matriarch, although that meant less.

If Kamal's cousin was the child of a woman who worked for the High Matriarch...

Zuli shook her head.

It didn't matter.

She didn't love Kamal's cousin. And love wasn't enough to allow her to marry Kamal.

All of it served as a reminder of the distance between them. Between the plains and the mountains was an impossible breach.

"There," Kamal said, drawing her away from her worries, "that should be your sister's flight."

Up ahead there was a golden-brown ship shaped like a dart, shimmering in the midday sun.

"My sister—" Zuli began.

"I know." Kamal squeezed her hand as he smiled. "You told me."

"It's been so long since I've seen her. I don't know..." *Anything*.

Not if Ada was well. Not how she'd survived in the harsh worlds away from her home sun. Not what her sister was thinking coming home.

There were so many unknowns.

As soon as the ground flyer stopped, Zuli opened the door. The transport ship was beautiful but unmarked, and there were armed guards wearing the yellow and tan of the planetary police standing under the ramp.

A shadow fell from the open side of the transport and Ada stepped out wearing a simple, single-layered, dark-brown sheath dress of rough linen. It fell off her like a sack, and yet Ada still looked beautiful. Her dark hair was pinned back, her face was free of makeup, and her feet were bare, but she was smiling.

"Zuli!" Ada held her arms wide as she reached the bottom of the ramp.

"Ada!" Zuli rushed her and hugged her close. "Oh! Ada! You didn't need to come home. Look at you." She ran her hand over the side of the rough dress. "It's so ugly!"

"Wait until I tell you about the fashions on Vivett Four. Branches were in style this season. I sat through a three-hour trade meeting wearing twigs in my hair and a dress with wooden beams in the sleeves." Ada walked across the burning tarmac quickly, but stopped to look at Kamal. "And this is?"

"Kamal of the Plains," Zuli said quickly. "A friend of mine from school."

Kamal bowed his head to Ada. "I'm trying to get upgraded from Friend to Husband. When the family decides on the date for Zuli's bridal night, I hope Older-Sister-Ada will remember me fondly?"

Ada laughed. "Oh, he's charming, Little One."

"Charming enough?" Kamal smiled hopefully.

Zuli opened the car door to hurry things along.

"Perhaps." Ada sat, moving gracefully as if the humiliation of landing barefoot and unadorned made no difference to her. "We are an unusual family," Ada said as Kamal and Zuli secured their seatbelts. "Born in the high peaks. Raised in adversity. A soft, gentle man from the Plains might find himself overwhelmed in our Household. You might do better with a lesser wife."

Covering shock with a coughing fit, Zuli shot her sister a look she hoped Ada would remember: SHUT UP. There was no way Ada had been gone so long she could ignore the basic protocols, or pretend she didn't understand the lofty titles his introduction hinted at.

Ada's eyes widened in mischievous delight.

"For my beloved Zuli, I can be as hard a man as she needs." Kamal looked up at the rearview mirror and winked back at Ada with a laugh.

"Kamal!" Zuli smacked his shoulder as her cheeks burned. "You shouldn't say such things around my family!"

"But, is it true, Little Sister?" Ada teased. "Have your tried your pretty boy from the Plains?"

"Ada!" Zuli turned in shock, certain her ears were turning deep red. "I'm going to die of embarrassment before my bridal night!"

Kamal patted her knee. "Don't worry, it's said with love. Your sister only wants the best husband for you, so do I. Your bridal night will be lovely."

Shaking her head, Zuli looked out the window at the passing desert, golden sand and blue sky, hoping to evade.

"When is the bridal night, exactly?" Kamal pressed.

"Oh, shush now," Ada said with a wave from the back seat. "This is not some illicit rendezvous between forbidden lovers. Our Zuli will have a proper bridal night. If your family is worthy, they'll be invited through the proper channels."

"If?" Kamal laughed, but he nodded. "Very well. Do you want my family name?"

"No," Ada said before Zuli could say yes. "My mother and I know all the matriarchs of the appropriate rank to court my sister. If you belong to one of those families, you'll be invited. If you aren't, you wouldn't be in consideration at all."

Zuli sank into her seat in morose silence. No matter how much Kamal loved her, the bride price was set: three rubies and a lifetime of regret.

Kyvaan's internal clock said it was midmorning, but dawn was only now pouring over the eastern mountains. Gold and cream light rippled over the soft curves of the distant hills, making the sky blush a delicate pink.

The desert was the land of dark gems and golden honey—at least that's what the poets said. As a younger man he'd snickered through the literary discussions that compared the thirsty desert to a dying man and the lush mountains to a beautiful woman. Now, in the opaline light of the rising sun, the golden light caressing the creamy curves of the world made him hungry for other curves. Desperate for the sight of sparkling black eyes and the challenge of dusky pink lips set in a ruthless smile.

On the patio outside the family's official rooms he stopped, breathing in the jasmine tea and forcing himself to stop thinking about how the gold of the morning light was the same as the gold of the label on the wine bottle. Or how the blue of the glasses had matched the blue of the distant mountain stones. Or how she hadn't been seen in public in weeks, curse the mysterious woman who toyed with his heart like a cat batting at a lizard.

Worries over where she may have gone tumbled over themselves in his mind as he sipped the floral tea.

Dala. He knew the name on her business license. The name that showed up in the headlines when she bought a company out from under him. The name that the rest of the universe knew her by.

But it wasn't her real name.

Legal name, perhaps, but not the one given to her at birth. There was too much of Tanar in her tactics and her talk for her to be anyone but a daughter of the world of gems. Too much anger and fury in her eyes when she'd heard his name that first fateful night.

The company for sale had been a small shipping firm, less than two dozen ships and only a handful more port contracts, but they were valuable ones. Captains and crews were part of the sale, promising at least three years of service each. The owners had wanted to ensure their company landed in good hands, so Kyvaan had gone to charm them.

He'd spent the night circulating with the same tepid wine in his glass, laughing at the same joke every quarter hour, patience waning. And then he'd seen her.

A vibrant blue dress that caught the hanging lights, the darkest brown hair, laughing black eyes. Her smile had made the whole torturous evening worth every second of boredom.

It had taken an hour to circle close enough to arrange an introduction, one that cost the promise not to go bidding on another company later in the week. He'd been introduced as a ruthless shark of a capitalist and she'd laughed.

They flirted, bantering about business, and then, somehow, it had all gone wrong. He'd mentioned his home planet of Tanar and lost her in a single breath. Something about his home repulsed her.

She'd hid it well, of course. But he saw it all the same and, stubborn man that he was, he'd wanted to win the truth from her.

Over the years he'd tried every tactic he knew of, even a few suggested by friends, and the most he'd ever gotten was an ongoing war over an unopened bottle of Ueenqi wine—the good stuff. A rich, purple liquid heady with the scent of black fruit and pepper. He'd invited her to share a glass after he'd acquired Iak Interstellar four years ago.

Except... he hadn't. He'd lost the bid at the last minute. When he'd gone to drink his disappointment away with the woman of his dreams, there'd been a bottle of the Ueenqi '37 and a note saying she'd love to have a meal sometime, but that night she was busy signing paperwork for a little company she'd purchased on a whim. A place called Iak. Perhaps he knew of it?

She'd beaten him at his own game.

His interest had gone from friendly interest to something more aggressive.

They met in public but never alone. When one took a company from the other, sniping acquisitions for their portfolio, the other was sent the bottle of wine.

Turning to lean against the white marble parapet of the dowager's inner fortress, he glared as the soft sunlight spilled over the blue glass of the cursed wine bottle.

Some day, some how, he was going to turn that bottle taunting him in his room to the woman he wanted. There was no one else like her. There never would be. And one day he'd find a way to get her alone for more than three minutes and explain why she should give him more than an enigmatic smile.

The hush of footsteps over stone in the parade ground pulled him away from his sleep-musings.

Down in the courtyard a lone figure in brown, flowing skirts strode down the main path as if she owned the place. Which... she did not.

That path was for the High Matriarch alone. Even her closest maids would have walked to the side, if they'd dared to be here unsummoned at all.

The gate to the rest of the palace, directly opposite his own apartments and towering several stories high, was still closed. While that was closed the only people allowed in this small refuge were the High Matriarch's family. Until his cousin married, that meant his cousin, himself, and Grandmother.

High above the parade ground, he fell into step with the woman below, trying to decipher her status.

This was the palace of Tanar; even the lowest maid in the fort wore thousands of gems. Rich tiger's eye and topaz. They wore little cornets pinned to their braids and there wasn't a single one in this city who wasn't qualified to teach economics to the greatest minds in the universe.

The women of Tanar were brilliant in every way.

This one, walking quietly through the early morning, before the guards had been called into the inner sanctum, moving like she had studied the layout...

Kyvaan set his teacup on the parapet and followed as his heart raced in panic.

The upper bailey curved around the parade grounds and led to the narrow stairs that gave the grandchildren access to the dowager's private gardens and rooms.

Grandmother wouldn't be up yet, not on a usual day.

He sped up as the stranger took the wide steps two at a time towards the garden.

"Kyvaan?" His cousin's sleepy voice pulled him up short. "What are you doing clattering through here? Do you know what time it is?"

"There's a woman here," he said, pulling his cousin along behind him, "but the guards aren't out yet."

Kamal peered over the parapet. "A serving woman. Probably a message. Or she might be one of the college women Grandma mentors."

"She's here very early for a student."

"There's no one strong enough to challenge us." Kamal stopped and stood his ground like a statue.

Kyvaan glared at him. "There is always someone strong enough to challenge us. If there weren't, we'd both have living parents."

"Grandmother wouldn't—"

"We're weak," Kyvaan said, quickening his steps. "There are no daughters left. No women to inherit if something happens to Grandmother. We're one assassin from ruin until you marry."

"Until *you* marry."

"You have someone who loves you," he said through grinding teeth. His cousin had a beautiful, lively, intelligent woman who seemed to adore him. All the letters from the university were filled with the most noxious praise of his paragon of perfection. He pushed past his cousin.

"One who won't tell me anything about herself except she's from the mountains."

"Mountain women are wily." Kyvaan came to the narrow stairs and rushed down them.

In the distance he saw his grandmother, resplendent in white and blue robes, step into the sunlight and hold her arms open for a welcoming hug.

The mysterious visitor bowed quickly and then rushed forward.

"See?" Kamal said, catching up. "A student."

He watched his grandmother welcome the stranger in like a missing daughter and felt his heart twist. Grandmother would love Dala. He could picture her smile as Dala moved from his embrace to the matriarch's. Surely those traded bottles and financial battles meant something. If Dala felt nothing for him, she would have cut off contact altogether. She'd certainly been direct with other men.

His cousin patted his back. "You worry overmuch."

"You worry too little." He watched for another moment to ensure himself his grandmother was safe with the interloper, then fell back into the shadows of the steps to give them privacy. "I thought she'd given up mentoring."

"Some of the older ones still visit."

"That one must have been poor as bones. Did you see her? No sparkle at all."

"Maybe her family trades in textiles? There's been a push the last few seasons for unornamented fabrics for daywear. To show off the weave and all."

Kyvaan wrinkled his nose at the thought. Tanar's wealth was in her gems that every foreign nation coveted. The last women he'd seen without gems on their gowns were the criminals being executed for the assassination of his parents and kin. An unhappy thought indeed.

He wanted to balance that pain with a stronger joy. *Dala*.

"Come on," Kamal said. "We're up early. Let's go find breakfast."

"Fine." His gaze lingered for a moment on the empty stone terrace, and, for only a breath, he thought he caught the smell of mountain lily and cardamom.

IT WAS THE HUSHED SOUNDED OF SILK-SLIPPERED STEPS THAT drew Zuli to the sheer cliff of the Worrier's Perch in the pre-dawn hours. That and her own fears.

She'd worked late into the night, selecting gifts for the cousins from her own closets. Beautiful silks and fine necklaces, the last of the wealth of the Yalsmons.

Today, the servants would be thanked and given two days away from the house while the family prepared for the bridal night. The lack of gifts for people who had been constant shadows in her life, overseeing everything from her first math lessons to her daily meals, was a gaping failure in her life.

Reaching out to help a wayward vine find the trellis, she saw Ada standing near the edge of the cliff, back to the river below, looking at the house with an inscrutable expression. "Ada?"

No response.

"Adalet!" Zuli said, loud enough to wake the birds in the trees.

Her sister turned, dark eyes fathomless and distant.

"Ada, what are you doing here?" Zuli crossed over a small strip of lawn to catch her sister. "Did you just wake up?"

Ada wasn't wearing sleeping clothes—probably. The simple browns of Ada's many-layered robe were made of silk and some shimmering fabric Zuli couldn't name. It was deceptively rich and fascinating while adhering strictly to the protocol of a banished woman, but it didn't look like sleepwear.

Taking her sister's arm, Zuli tugged her away from the cliff. "You're up early."

"My body hasn't adjusted to the time zones yet. It feels like midday." Ada flashed her a smile.

"Midday is a bad time for worrying." Especially near a steep and deadly drop.

"Worrying?" Confusion crossed Ada's face and her eyes flicked from Zuli to something beyond.

Zuli turned. At the very edge of the horizon, a golden flyer zipped along the path above the raging river. "You went somewhere? Alone?"

"Little One, I did live on this planet most my life. I still have friends. Since my sojourn is brief, and I couldn't sleep any more this morning, I thought it was best to use my time renewing old ties."

"Still," Zuli said, "wouldn't it be better to take someone with you? Mother? Me? Even Father?"

"I met someone for morning tea and some light gossip." Ada laughed. "Don't worry about me! Really, Zuli, I'm not suffering. I am here to see your bridal night, wish you well, and finish the terms of my banishment. I have not picked up assassin's skills while I was away. I won't break and cry on the ground as you walk to a married life. I'm excited to be here."

At least one of them wasn't going to break and cry as Zuli married Jonthir.

Zuli smiled despite the impending doom. "Good. Then come in and let's prepare. The cousins are only an hour or two away and it's time to thank the household staff."

They only took a few steps toward the house before Ada stopped moving.

"Is there a problem?" Zuli asked. "Would you rather not attend?"

"No," Ada said slowly, "but I wonder if I could impose, ever so slightly, on your joy. I know it isn't appropriate for a sister to pick gifts for anyone. It's terribly gauche." Ada looked at the brown stones of the garden path smoothed by centuries of hurrying feet. "It's just that I never had a chance to thank anyone. I never got as far as the gifting before my bridal night, and I wondered if you'd allow me to supplement your own gifts. Add just a few of my own. No one ever need know they were from me. You can take all the credit. But it would put my heart at peace."

Zuli laughed. "I have little enough to give as it is. We're poor, Ada. Fortunes fall."

"Fortunes fall so that they may rise again," her sister chided. "If you are going to quote the great matriarchs, quote them correctly, Little One."

"I value your teaching, Elder Sister," Zuli replied mockingly, bowing her head as if the first ships had just made landfall.

Clicking her tongue, Ada took Zuli's arm. "Come now, will you let me add a few boxes to the trove?"

"What trove? What boxes? You came to the planet with nothing but the tiny pouch I embroidered for you all those years ago. What did you have hidden in there?"

"Candy," Zuli said promptly. "But my time abroad has not been hopeless nor unfruitful. I had a business partner going this way and paid them to bring a few things to place in storage."

"Ada!" Even knowing they were in the family garden far from prying eyes, Zuli looked around in dread. "You can't own anything when you return from exile. Those are the terms. You may do whatever you wish while you are away, but if you are to return it must be owning nothing but the clothes on your back as you dance barefoot at a bride's celebration. If the judge's council learns you owned property when you landed they'll seize it and permanently banish you! Mother's heart would break! Mine would break!"

"I don't own anything." Ada's forehead wrinkled in honest confusion. "I covered the cost of shipping for some items coming to the planet, and I purchased them originally, but ownership was transferred. Everything I owned was sold off last month. I don't even have a rental agreement any more. I sold off my shares in every company, transferred ownership from myself to business associates, gave away every stitch of clothing except my travel dress."

"Where did you get this?" Zuli asked, picking at the fluttery robe Ada was wearing.

"Mother gave it to me last night."

"It's off-world fabric."

Ada shrugged. "And? Just because the law says I couldn't contact my maternal line doesn't mean I couldn't make introductions and allow other people to contact my home. So I dropped mother's name in the ears of people looking to expand." Ada lifted her hands in surrender to the universe. "That is their business. I only said a name. Nothing more. Nothing illegal, certainly."

Zuli narrowed her eyes and scrutinized her sister's guileless face. There was no lie in her eyes. No hesitation in her voice. Nothing that would say Ada had been sneaky, but that in and of itself was telling. "You've done business while away?"

"Oh, yes. Of course! I needed to make a living somehow."

"You left with nothing."

"A friend of an old mentor reached out once I was out of the system. They needed some help, and it paid well and quickly."

"How has business been?"

"Profitable until recently. Divesting of everything was a shame."

"You shouldn't have come," Zuli said. "You should have stayed there, prosperous and profitable. Safe and secure."

Ada squeezed her into a hug. "Or I could be here and see you married well. Come now, I am your beloved older sister. Would I leave you poor and wanting when I had so much? I gave it all away, but you never asked who I gave it to. Now, let's go wish the servants well, thank them for their service, and prepare for the cousins. We have a busy day and not a small number of gifts."

With a smile, Ada pushed Zuli ahead into the cool shadows of the house and down the back hall to where the servants were gathered before mother's throne. It was a small room lined with cupboards, illuminated by skylights and two grand stained-glass windows on either side of the small dais where two wooden thrones sat.

Mother was there wearing bronze and blue, a small, golden coronet pinned at the center of her head with a gauzy, midnight blue veil falling over her dark tresses. Father was beside her in a matching suit, three golden earrings on the upper curl of his right ear.

The room had once been a training room for the household guard, and a workout room for her and Ada when they were young. Now all of the servants fit inside, six to either side standing in neat line. They wore the dark brown livery of the house, accented by sapphires and shots of golden thread.

In the center of the room were boxes, trunks really, made of rare golden eaglewood and carved with scenes from fairytales. The spicy scent of the wood perfumed the air and reminded Zuli of the First Summer Festival in the high mountains.

"Azuli," Mother said, "youngest of my line, bright star of my heavens, great scholar of my people, I have called my household together today to honor you."

The traditional words felt heavy on her shoulders. "Beloved Mother," Zuli knelt in front of the dais, "creator of life, giver of all good gifts, honored beyond time and measure, it is I who should give honor and thanks. Your household raised me in splendor and glory. Your wisdom created opportunities for me. Your hands grew wrinkled and old caring for me. Beloved Mother, allow me to give a few gifts to these, your honored hands."

"As you will it, daughter mine."

Her heart felt light as she stood, or maybe just her head. At Ada's insistence she'd left her silks and necklaces behind, bringing nothing but poor words of praise for the people who helped raise her. And it would have been enough. The whole house had fallen and suffered together. Mother had never turned cruel or abandoned her people, even as her own fortunes fell and opportunities faded.

"Little One," Ada said softly, "I've prepared the list as you wished." She held out a small, blue tablet with a description of each trunk and servant before fading back into the shadows.

"Thank you, Sister Sweetest." She couldn't let the confusion show on her face. This was her first true show of strength, giving the servants presents she chose herself, but Ada had done the work and the guilt made Zuli's heart cold.

Focusing on the list, Zuli smiled at the youngest servant, a girl of fourteen whose family's misfortunes meant they could not afford schooling for her. The Yalsmon family had taken her in at age ten to run errands and sweep floors in exchange for paying for her tuition.

"Falladah," Zuli said, "youngest of my mother's hands, the youthful joy of our hearts, you receive the first and smallest of gifts."

Ada pushed a trunk as long as Zuli's leg over on a grav-lift that sagged under the weight.

With a nod of encouragement from Zuli, Falladah opened the trunk. There was a dress dripping with more gems than Zuli's own bridal gown, more cloth, art, statues, papers.

Zuli swallowed hard and turned back to the tablet. "In addition to this small gift—" she was going to discuss the size of gifts with Ada later "—I wish to pay for your university tuition in full, for any university you wish, and have sent to your mother three beneficial business contacts that I hope will grow your family."

Three?

THREE???

The contents of the trunk alone would be enough to change the Yalsmons' status. Three good business tips would allow them to rebuild in under a decade. Yet Ada was handing this away for *free*?

Zuli shot her sister a disapproving look.

Ada smiled beatifically.

"Next, dear Greshi," Zuli said, "who has served to strengthen the stones of the house and kept us safe from storm and fire..."

The whole list was the same. Every trunk revealing more extravagant gifts. Every servant given a lifetime or two of wealth and chance.

By the time the cousins arrived and Zuli saw the dresses Ada had prepared for them, she was numb. In under three hours Ada had raised everyone under her family's protection from Noted or Esteemed to Significant or better.

Her cousins were still marveling over their good fortune and giggling with delight as Ada led Zuli away to her private rooms and a small luncheon on the patio near the garden waterfall.

"Are you well, Little One?" Ada asked as she poured a pink hibiscus tea.

"I'm in shock!" Zuli drained her cup in a single swallow and set it down for Ada to refill. "You gave mother's secretary two small businesses, the contract swept out from her rival's hands, and enough money to ensure her grandchildren all marry well! The last person to give so much as a bride became High Matriarch!"

"Yes," Ada said, refilling the cup, "I do realize it seems a bit extravagant after so many years of cautious spending. This is how investments work, though. In time, they pay off. It is traditional to give your servants between one and ten percent of your surplus as a bride."

"You gave old Yellini a quarter of our profit!"

Ada sat down, the plain robe jumping like startled grasshoppers with every move. "I gave her three percent of your current wealth. It'll be less than one percent in two weeks."

"What?" That couldn't be right. Her head swam at the miscalculation. How could Ada miscalculate so badly?

"My gifts to you," Ada said, "are on the last page of the memo. The assessment is in two days and the whole universe will know, but tomorrow night you are a bride, and you should know your worth. We were poor, because I had to pay the price of Esko's attack. Because I was too prideful to allow myself to submit to such a man. Because I dared think myself worthy of more than the son of a rich woman.

"You suffered for it, and I promised myself I would not let you suffer long. Everything I did these past five years was for you. You will go out there tomorrow night as one of the wealthiest women on the planet. Let your suitors throw their rubies at you. Let them try to get themselves a bargain wife because they don't know your true worth. You know your worth, and that's all that matters."

"I still can't tell Kamal." Zuli pushed the plate of dainty

cookies aside and skimmed the pages. "His family would never allow such a thing. I don't even know who they are."

"Mother is clever," Ada said encouragingly. "Don't you think she'll reach out? It won't be only men from the local village coming to see you."

Zuli smiled wanly. "But it won't be Kamal either. Even if I told him better days were coming, which would break all etiquette and tradition, do you think his family would come?" Her heart broke in bitter, jagged pieces once again. "They'll look at our assessment from after your banishment and think I'm worthless! If we could push the bridal night back a week we—"

"We would have every fortune hunter in the six nearest systems hunting you down. Esko isn't the only one whose family's money comes from attacking brides. This is better. If someone comes tomorrow you know they want you, not the wealth you have."

"It's worse! Kamal won't be there."

"Perhaps he will, perhaps he won't. I don't know all of mother's connections. If he is, wonderful, all is happiness and joy. If he isn't, alas, you don't need to choose a groom. You can wait a year and propose to him then."

"As if his family will wait a year. He's the highest ranked male scholar on the planet!"

"Second highest."

"Highest."

"Second," Ada said firmly. "He has a cousin who scored better when he graduated seven years ago."

Zuli felt her soul leave her body. "He has a cousin?"

"Yes." Ada picked up a delicate lavender cookie and bit it in half.

"How do you know he has a cousin? We don't even know his family line!"

Ada's eyes went wide. "We don't?" she asked around a mouthful of crumbs.

"I don't."

"Hmm." Ada nodded. "Interesting."

"Ada!"

Her sister stood in a flurry of too-light fabric. "Enjoy your lunch, Little One. I need to go wait on mother and the aunties while the servants are away. Enjoy the cookies!" Ada dropped a quick kiss on her head and ran away.

Friends in the city? Old contacts? Cousin?

Ada had been down there hunting for Kamal's family?

The possibility cleared her head. *Maybe.*

Zuli picked up her tea again and watched the water pour over the rocks to the garden pond where the blush-pink lilies danced in the current. Maybe—just maybe—tomorrow night wouldn't be so bad after all.

A SWOLLEN, GIBBOUS MOON HUNG OVER THE PALACE GARDENS, making the night-blooming flowers glow like ethereal pearls on wine-dark vines. Candles flickered in the desert wind, bringing in the scent of the city and the spaceport beyond.

Kyvaan held a wineglass full of water up to the starlight and very carefully did not smash it against the rocks in frustration. A day spent checking every record, contacting every resource he had on planet, chasing down every crumb of information, and still all he had was smoke and the memory of lily perfume.

"Why are we not opening the wine?" his cousin demanded from the table behind him.

After hours of fruitless searching, Kyvaan had given in to the comforts of home and arranged a dinner on the garden terrace. His cousin, still sulking after an unhappy afternoon waiting for news about his wished-for wife, had joined him. It wasn't actually helping his mood.

His cousin reached for the forbidden bottle. "Come on. I'm still too sober."

"No. I'm saving it. I'll pack it in the morning." He rescued the bottle and poured his cousin some water.

"Why are you leaving so soon?"

"Because I can't find what I'm looking for here and two counselors have already reached out to me to invite me to family events next week. I need to get off planet before I'm trapped."

"Trapped?" A deep alto voice cut through the night like the smell of burning asphalt.

Kyvaan and his cousin shot to their feet. "Grandmama."

She waved them down as she swept in, her skirt heavy with gold-thread embroidery and diamonds. Fire opals dotted her white hair, glittering more than any off-world crown. "You're leaving?"

"That was the plan," Kyvaan said. Emphasis on the was, because Grandmother had a habit of overruling his plans.

"You've barely spent any time at all here. Not even a week."

His cousin held a chair out for Grandmother.

They didn't sit until she gestured for them to join her.

"I came home on business," Kyvaan said. "There was no other reason to stay."

"Seeing your family isn't reason enough?"

Kyvaan glanced at his cousin, who was carefully avoiding eye contact. "You're busy. My cousin is—"

"Graduated," Grandmother said. "He is free as any unmarried man running his mother's business. Are your off-world contacts so much more interesting than family matters?"

"Kyvaan is chasing a woman," his cousin offered helpfully.

Violence had never been Kyvaan's preferred method of dealing with rivals, but his cousin's willingness to sacrifice him to the post-graduation bridal bazaar had to be countered. He settled back in his chair, radiating confidence. "I thought my cousin needed less distraction, and competition. He's chasing someone from school. A lady of White River."

"Oh?" Grandmother turned on his cousin with a slow, predatorial smile. "You have not mentioned this lovely daughter of White River before. Is she a new affection?"

"No, she's the same one I spoke to you about last summer and the summer before. We've been—" His cousin fumbled for an appropriate term, cheeks turning red.

"Sweethearts?" Grandmother suggested.

His cousin nodded weakly. "Yes, sweethearts, for three years now. She's the only woman I've worked to court. We've partnered on multiple projects. She's brilliant. A fine mind, excellent at investments, thoroughly educated on arts and maths. You'll adore her."

"When do I get to meet her?"

It was Kyvaan's turn to look away while his cousin dug himself out of this trap.

"Ah, well, the lady is a little shy," his cousin said. "Her name is Zuli, of White River, and she hasn't arranged the bridal night yet."

"Hasn't arranged or hasn't invited you?" Trust Grandmama to strike at the heart of the problem.

"Her sister intends to send an invite."

That was news. Kyvaan looked up with interest. "You met her sister?"

His cousin nodded. "Earlier this week, when I ran out to go meet someone? I borrowed your pass to get into the port to collect her."

"She was off planet?" Kyvaan frowned. Very few women traveled off-planet, and almost never alone. If his cousin's beloved Zuli had family traveling out of the system, she might be a more likely match than her reticence suggested.

"What did the sister say?" Grandmother asked.

"That her family's matriarchs would reach out to ours if they thought the match was beneficial." His cousin's expression was downcast at the thought.

"Which they won't," Kyvaan said, "because you introduced yourself as Kamal from the Plains so they have no idea who you are."

"There were safety concerns," his cousin muttered.

The two of them had been with Grandmother the night their family's convoy had been attacked. Kyvaan's two sisters, his parents, and Kamal's parents, all killed in the same blast. Grief had taught them to be circumspect, to guard their identities closely. Survival came at the price of intimacy and friendship.

"Well, either the girl is as clever as you think and her mother will contact me, or she won't."

"Would you accept a woman of a lesser rank as his wife?" Kyvaan asked. He hadn't planned on using his cousin's situation as bait, but if it got him the answer he needed, his cousin could wriggle.

Grandmother's eyes softened. "For you two to have happiness, I will accept anyone. My dear daughters are dead. I will not lose the last of my bloodline to petty concerns over a mother's wealth. Power can be gained. Cunning can be taught. Wealth can be accumulated over a lifetime of work. But happiness is not for sale to any coin. It is one of the few things I cannot command or provide with a wave of my hand. You must make it yourself."

His cousin slumped with relief.

"However, while you wait and before Kyvaan leaves," Grandmother said, "you will both do me the courtesy of attending a bridal night with me tomorrow."

"No!" The protest was in unison.

"You will do well to observe a bridal night before you attend your lady's," Grandmother told his cousin. Then she turned to him. "Why are you objecting? You've mentioned no one."

Kyvaan swallowed a crude word. "There is a woman I met off-world."

His grandmother's eyebrows went up in surprise. "A woman better than all the daughters of the sun you were born under? That seems highly unlikely."

"I think she was Tanar trained. Probably raised here. Possibly exiled, or perhaps her family was," he admitted slowly. This was tricky ground and rushing could lead to his doom far too easily. "She recently made some sales and deals that sounded like they had ties to Tanar. I came to research them."

"What did you learn?" The imperious command that followed every mistake since he was old enough to toddle.

Kyvaan shook his head. "Very little, Grandmother. She covered her tracks well. I know the names, but they're hard to track using my sources."

"Why didn't you come to me?"

"Grandmother?" He shook his head in confusion.

"My dear boy, did you even stop to consider asking me for help?"

"I...." He trailed off as his cousin hid a snicker.

"Do you really want to find her?"

"Yes."

"What will you do when you find her?"

He pressed his lips together as he considered his grandmother's unspoken offer. "What is the help worth to you?"

"Two days," his grandmother said. "Non-negotiable. Stay two more days on planet and attend the bridal night with me and your cousin. After that, I will use every resource I have to track down this mysterious woman for you."

"Does she have a name?" his cousin asked.

"Do you have a counter-offer?" Kyvaan asked.

"If I know her, take me with you off planet," his cousin said. "We leave tonight. If I can't go to Zuli's bridal night, I'll go to none."

His grandmother watched them, interested but unthreatened.

"Her name is Dala."

His grandmother smirked and held out a hand for Kamal to bid.

His cousin shook his head. "I don't know her by name."

"Then your only recourse is to come with me or try your luck off world," Grandmother said.

"I'm not bidding on the bride," Kyvaan said. "I'll attend with you. I will stay the two days. But I will make no matches in those two days and enter into no agreements."

"You don't want to offer her your forbidden wine?" his cousin teased, tapping the blue and gold bottle of Ueenqi wine.

"No. I'm offering my presence, nothing more."

"Accepted," Grandmother said. "I will see you both at noon tomorrow, dressed appropriately."

His cousin reached for the open bottle of champagne. "Yes, Grandmother. Accepted."

Kyvaan nodded. "Accepted."

She smiled. "Good. Then I have all I want."

Fireflies drifted through the inner courtyard like wayward stars, twinkling and dancing through the replanted garden. Zuli stood at the Worrier's Perch, mind turning over everything that had happened in the past few days.

The outer courtyard was set, tables arranged with copper silk tablecloths and an ocean of blue lanterns illuminating the magnolia trees that had just started to bloom white this morning. Already she could hear the murmur of guests entering the forecourt. Jonthir and his friends had arrived early to get the best seat up front. His mother and sisters were, no doubt, pointedly absent. Other neighbors were coming as well. Her mother's old friends. Even a few of her father's friends.

To the guests streaming through the front gate she was nothing more than an impoverished bride, her value coming from her ties to her mother, not in who she was alone.

Behind the curtains hung between pillars of the front portico, the world was dizzyingly different. Her cousins and the maids were all dressed beautifully, glimmering in gold, gems, and imported silk. Only the High Matriarch could dress her house better, and not by much.

The air smelled of rich perfumes, delicate silks, and gold. Every millimeter of her gown was stitched with gold, jewels, and rare off-world pearls. She touched a carved eaglewood button, the cost of import alone more than the three rubies Jonthir planned to offer her. Even in her wildest childhood fancies she had never dreamed of having a bride's night this grand.

And still, her heart hammered.

Kamal wouldn't be there.

Every little girl dreamed of finding her perfect match, and to see him waiting on her bridal night when she went to choose a husband. There were countless stories about it. A million songs. Ten million poems.

But her family was too meager, too insubstantial, to track him down or invite his family. She could have asked him directly, sent him a hint. But that would forever taint the relationship between her and the women in his life.

The mother should be invited. Or aunt. Or grand-mother. Or sister. Whatever woman was welcoming her as an ally after the match was made.

So the dream wouldn't come true.

She'd wait the year. If Kamal was still unwed, they could still have a private match. They could still be together. They just needed to survive a year apart.

"Little One?" Her sister's voice hung in the air like her lily perfume.

"I'm here."

"Why are you hiding in the dark?" Ada's light, bare-footed steps hurried across the flagstones. "Are you all right?"

"I'm just... It's so much, Ada! Last week I thought I would trade my life for three rubies and protection for the cousins. Today I'm going to trade my wealth for another year of being without a husband. I should be happy. I am happy. It's only... A part of me still wants the storybook ending. The happily ever after. The perfect match."

"Oh! Zuli!" Ada wrapped her arms around her in a sisterly hug. "You deserve that, Sweet One. You do. But you can't have the fairytale ending without the ending.

"You have to go out there and try. Otherwise the story is unfinished. Go out there. Show the world who Azuli Yalsmon truly is. Be proud of yourself and your family. Be proud of all you've done. Let the story write itself. All you need to do tonight is just be yourself."

Zuli squeezed her sister, trying hard not to cry.

"Tonight is your night, Zuli. Tonight anything can happen."

"Thank you. For everything."

"Anytime." Ada gave her one more tight squeeze and then stepped back, the unadorned silk falling off her like a river of gold. "Now, are you ready to destroy a man's ego, leave his awful sister weeping in the dirt, and show the world who you truly are?"

Zuli straightened her gem-encrusted skirt, tapping the heavy diamond designed to peel away at a touch. "I am."

"Then let's go meet the potential grooms."

THE MATRIARCH'S VEHICLE OF CHOICE WAS A DUSKY BLUE transport in a style that had been popular twenty years ago. It looked aged, but respectably cared for, as if it belonged to a much humbler woman. Her guards in ashy gray linen and pewter, decorated with unobtrusive diamond and sapphire, arrived ahead of them, arranged a discreet landing zone, and saw them through an empty alley to the rear entrance of the house meant for close family friends.

Ever mindful of past tragedy, Kyvaan scanned the low roofs of the neighboring houses, searching for trouble. On either side of the narrow valley the mountain peaks loomed, and under the murmur of the guards' movements he heard the rushing of the distant river echoing in the steep drop-off behind the house.

A silver-haired guard smiled as he approached. "The area is clear. No one but the family is expecting your arrival and none of the guests have been informed."

"Good. We'll see if anyone recognizes Grandmama." Most wouldn't. Dressed in the midnight-blue silk and teal sapphires, they were indistinguishable from any other well-led house. Wealthy, but only the silk, organic and unproduceable by terraforming machines, hinted at how wealthy.

If the Matriarch had wanted shock and awe, she would have worn blue gold, with pearls and amber, wood beads and jet, ammolite and coral. The exotic and the extraordinary.

They quietly approached a house in the mountain style, with various outbuildings connected by small gardens and surrounded by a shoulder-high fence lined with ancient trees. The gate to the private entrance was lined with low, flowering shrubs that smelled of a lemony herb meant to keep insects away. A young girl appeared at the doorway wearing copper-and-gold silks, dotted with amber and wood. Golden pearls were woven into her black braids between diamond beads.

It was clear at a glance that, no matter how humble the house was, the family within was equal to the Matriarch and her kin.

"They sent the little sister," his cousin whispered in his ear. "How do you think the older one looks?"

The little sister was too young to have a woman's lines in face or body, but her eyes were well rounded and her cheekbones promising.

"Not a great beauty, but tolerable." The memory of Dala taunted him. Her beauty was in her wit and cunning even more than her black eyes and softly tempting lips. Perhaps tonight's lucky groom would be blessed with half that cunning in the bride hosting the event tonight.

"Matriarch, kin." The young girl nodded to them in a polite-but-slightly-lower-subservient way. "I am Falladah, maid of this house. M'lady Yalsmon asked me to show you directly to your seats at the back of the garden. I will see to your needs directly with the help of the bride's sister."

"Maid?" His cousin looked at him in surprise.

The girl blinked up at them, sudden fear in her eyes. "Yes. Is that all right?"

"It's perfectly fine, dear one," Grandmother said, laying a comforting hand on the girl's shoulder. "How long have you worked for the Yalsmons?"

"They took me in four years ago. Mama thought I should take some tutoring here, since school was costly after her surgery. Matriarch Yalsmon has been very good to me and seen to my education. The bride's gift to me was my university tuition, plus three business contacts for my family, and some art along with some other small things. I'll return to school after the wedding season. My sister too. The bride was very generous."

"That is good to hear." Grandmother patted her on the back and shooed her inside. "A woman should always get as much education as she can. A man too, since he will need to help his wife and raise their children well."

"I will remember you said such, Matriarch," the little girl said with perfect diplomacy.

Kyvaan nudged his cousin and mouthed the word, "Yalsmon?"

His cousin shook his head. "Never heard of them."

Intriguing. The family was wealthy enough to dress their servants better than most Grand house matrons, influential enough to invite the High Matriarch to an event without hesitation, yet reclusive to the point that their name had never come to his ears.

The girl in pearls led them through a magnolia-scented breezeway, past a night garden with a quiet fountain surrounded by water lilies, through a set of arches where tiled floors with imported fossil leaves imprinted sprawled underfoot, to the reception courtyard fully lit and glittering in anticipation of the bride's arrival.

They entered the garden near the stage where the bride would stand, on the far side from the entry gate. The woman's family sat at a curving table decorated in bronze —no, Kyvaan studied it at a distance and saw river stone had been used to build a full table with a trench of water filled with white fish, blooming lotuses, and candles.

Smaller round tables with bronze and copper cloths were spread out across the courtyard under the branches of a great tree hung with blue lanterns. More strings of lights and lanterns ran the length of the courtyard, giving the illusion of being under a glowing wave.

"Here is your table," the girl said, showing them a small table in a shadowed corner, almost hidden from view. It was a seat meant for an observer, not a bidder.

His cousin's shoulders relaxed as the realization hit home. No one was going to announce them or recognize them. No one was going to force their hand and require a bid.

"This is quite lovely," Grandmother said as she sat.

"Matriarch Yalsmon has done everything possible to ensure her daughter has a happy bridal night. Her first daughter—" The maid grimaced.

Grandmother nodded. "I understand. I'm aware of the unpleasantness. Deeply troubling, all around. But I trust the elder sister bears no ill will to the younger?"

"Oh, no, Matriarch! M'lady Yalsmon is the perfect sister! She fully supports the bride and is so happy for her! She's shown me how to be a better older sister. I am working to make sure my younger sisters will have the same support when they are grown. They are very young though, so I have time to grow some businesses for them."

"As one should," the Matriarch agreed. "Thank you for everything, please, don't feel you need to hover, we require very little."

The girl nodded and hurried away, pointedly ignoring the guards taking station in the darkness along the wall.

"What an energetic child," Grandmother said. "I don't doubt she'll be on the council someday."

"I've never heard any of my friends in university saying they started as maids. Is that common in the mountains?" His cousin poured water from a crystal decanter as he spoke.

"No," Grandmother said. "Serving is usually the work of the poor and the motherless. When there are no aunts or grandmothers, sometimes a father will find a family willing to tutor a girl. The poorer families who must work and can't afford schooling hope to find an employer willing to let them learn from watching. She had the good fortune to land with a family able to lift her beyond her birth."

"I can't imagine they'll keep much staff if they keep sending them away to schools," Kyvaan said, accepting a drink. The argument over whether schooling should be free to all was centuries old and not worth ruining the peace of the evening over.

"My people only work a season or two with me," Grandmother said. "Then they go on to school and running businesses of their own. A clever person can learn much when working in even menial tasks."

A shadow fell over them as the breeze brought the scent of cardamom and lilies from the night garden. "Wine?"

"Yes, please." His cousin held a glass up for the hovering servant.

Kyvaan and grandmother followed suit.

"Mmm!" His grandmother murmured in pleasure. "Ueenqi '37! I haven't had this in ages! How delightful. I didn't realize there were any more bottles available."

A slender hand placed an open bottle of Ueenqi wine in front of him. The blue-and-gold label held his attention a fraction of a second too long. When he looked up, the woman was gone in a wave of unadorned gold silk and the fragrance of cardamom.

ZULI PEEKED BETWEEN THE HEAVY, BLACK VELVET CURTAINS dividing the atrium and breezeway from the torch-lit stage on the portico.

Jonthir, his three cousins, and several friends sat at the center table, laughing as they drank the worst wine Ada could find. They'd taken no notice of the decorations, or had assumed they were traditional family heirlooms that Jonthir's kin would profit from soon.

Once more she reviewed the list of assets to be announced when she walked on stage.

Somehow Ada had done the impossible. Their family wasn't simply restored, they were reborn, uplifted, powerful. Her mother now held enough wealth that a council invite would be hers for the asking. Zuli's cousins were sitting comfortably, knowing they could freely marry anyone on the planet. And Zuli was free to marry no one at all.

The cool evening air tasted of magnolia and lily. She breathed it in, shook off the last of her worries, and walked onto the stage.

Music swelled from the hidden speakers. With a step, she silenced it, bringing every eye to her.

"Welcome, friends, family, and new acquaintances." She nodded to the shadowed tables in the back where her mother and aunt's friends were seated. "I am Azuli Yalsmon, second daughter of Azuri Yalsmon. To my marriage I bring my mother's fortune, her businesses and lands, sixteen off-world contacts, two corporations, and fifty-one percent of the planet Nykiinos, plus the birth-wealth of my dowry."

The lights moved to catch the glimmer of silk and the gems on her dress.

"At this time, I welcome all bids from men who think they are my equal. I am looking for a husband from a well-respected family who can support my growth, my companies, and my children. Jonthir, son of Eyoti of House Thelwun, your sisters have talked about me much on the public forums." Her smile turned sharp. "I understand you have an offer?"

The spotlight fell on a sweating Jonthir. He wore a simple set of slacks and a plain gray t-shirt. It was an insult to show up in such casual clothes with no women kin to welcome her.

"Do you still wish to make an offer?" Zuli asked again, her voice honeyed poison.

"Of course, sweet Azuli." Jonthir stood. "My heart is yours. My family is humble, but let me offer you three red rubies of the river where I first fell in love with you." He held out his hand with three stones smaller than her pinkie nail, but polished, which was a step up from the raw stone she'd been expecting.

Zuli studied them in silence.

Jonthir tried to smile.

"Three rubies?" She caught his eyes and held him there. "I bring off-world contracts, access to mining rights, a moon, half a planet, and a wealth that would make the High Matriarch pleased, and you offer me three rubies?"

"Rubies and wealth are..." Jonthir glanced at his kin for support. "They are so little. So very little. What I have for you is true affection. True love. Is—is—is not love worth more than rubies?"

"Love? Without the support of your sisters or mother? Love that brings you here looking like you forgot this was a bridal night?" Zuli shook her head as she peeled the diamond off her skirt. "Here. You are dear neighbors. I've known you many years. Take this gem, and bring your mother home wealth that will ensure her daughters can marry well. Your offer is too small for me, but perhaps another woman will find your reduced circumstances endearing."

Zuli dropped the diamond in Jonthir's hand and turned away, heart soaring.

Shocked silence settled over the gardens and she drank it in.

It was over.

Again, she took a deep breath and turned to the audience, dazzling them with a smile. "Does anyone else have an offer?"

"Beloved Azuli," a voice called from the left, "I am Onmar, son of Matriarch Drellin Kley of House Kley. I offer you one fifth of my mother's businesses, two houses, a fine new flyer for you and your parents, beautiful statues imported from Halerryn in the Vega System. I will ensure your days are filled with joy and the laughter of as many children as you want."

"Zuli!" Another voice shot up from a neighboring table. "Let me offer you half my mother's businesses."

More men stood. Sisters. Mothers. They threw businesses and wealth at her, and it washed over her like a gentle spring breeze.

She was free.

"Zuli!" Kamal froze with his glass halfway to his lips.

Kyvaan raised an eyebrow and watched the bride dismissing offers out of hand.

"Grandmother!" His cousin turned, outrage and betrayal on his face.

"What?" Grandmother held up her hands. "I've known the family for years! I do business with her older sister. Is it wrong to bring you?"

"Ada said she'd ask my family. I didn't think she meant it!" His cousin set his glass down very carefully while seeming to calmly panic. "Grandma!"

"What?" Again the Matriarch shrugged as if nothing had changed. "Adalet is a good big sister and a sweet child.

Why wouldn't I honor her request to come? After all, she came in person to ask me."

Adalet. Adala. *Dala.*

His breath caught. He hadn't been dreaming that morning on the terrace. It had been Dala in his grandmother's palace. Dala in her lily-and-cardamom perfume. Dala placing a bottle of opened wine in front of him as a peace offering.

Kyvaan searched the darkness for the plain bronze silk.

"Grandmother!" Kamal sounded desperate. "The match! Can I bid?"

"I promised I wouldn't force you," Grandmother said with a soft smile, "but I didn't say you couldn't bid at all. Offer her one of the armed trade ships too. A gift from your matriarch."

"And the other half of the planet," Kyvaan said. Dala either sold her half to the bride or gifted it to the family. "My wedding gift to you both."

Kamal stood, triggering a small spotlight. "Zuli."

The bridal bidding fell quiet.

Zuli's eyes went wide with shock.

"Zuli, I offer you all of my mother's companies and assets. For you and any children we may have. With the blessing of my grandmother, Matriarch of my family, I offer you an armed merchant ship and the other forty-nine percent of the planet Nykiinos. I have holds in Rishyr, Helvet, and Yom Systems, with export licenses, as well as contacts in seventeen major spaceports."

Kamal.

It was impossible. It had to be... unless.

Zuli searched the shadows for Ada. Had her sister known who his family was after all?

It had to be dream, but Kamal was standing there, at a table in the back next to an older woman and a man who might be kin. "Kamal of the Plains."

Walking closer she recognized the woman, noticed the guards in blue and pewter hidden in the shadows of the trees. "High Matriarch." Zuli inclined her head.

"You are a beautiful bride." The High Matriarch, resplendent in midnight silk and teal sapphires, smiled and nodded back. "My grandson would make a good catch, don't you think?"

"I offer you naming rights for all our children," Kamal continued. "Override on home decor. Please, Zuli...."

She studied him in serene silence. It seemed too like a dream, him standing there in a blue suit that perfectly matched her copper gown, love in his eyes. She was afraid that if she moved she'd wake up, trapped in a horrible world where none of this was real.

A breeze with the scent of her mother's herb garden cut through the unreality, ruffling the magnolias overhead and making the candlelight dance.

"Zuli," Kamal said, almost reaching for her.

"That is a fine opening offer," she agreed as slowly as the petals drifting from the tree overhead. "But anyone can offer me ships and businesses. What can you give me that no one else has?"

"My heart," Kamal said without hesitation, taking her hand with a smile. "My enduring love. I will spend my life making you happy, supporting you, advising you, encouraging you."

"Children?" Zuli shot back. "Will you help me raise them? Teach them? Protect them?"

"Yes, as many as you want. Anything you want."

She glanced at the table. The woman beside Kamal in sapphires and silk smiled at her. "High Matriarch," Zuli bowed her head in respect, "will I have your support and tutelage if I accept your grandson?"

"You will."

"I want everything," Zuli said to Kamal. "I want a hundred lifetimes with you and only you."

"I will do everything to give you that," Kamal promised.

Tears blurred her vision. "I accept your proposal."

Confused applause and whispers broke out across the courtyard. The lights were only now rising in the corner, and people only starting to guess who she was speaking with.

Zuli wiped the tears away hastily. "High Matriarch, please, allow me to bring my family to greet you."

"Nonsense child, the groom's family greets the parents of the bride. That is how it has always been done."

"Surely the High Matriarch—"

"—will rise to greet her granddaughter's mother," the High Matriarch said firmly. "Your parents have raised an excellent daughter, cunning and wise. I should show them the proper respect for their fine work the same way my daughters' grooms' parents bowed to me on their bridal nights."

The whispers behind them were reaching a fevered pitch. People had recognized Kamal and the High Matriarch.

"Are you happy?" Kamal whispered as he took her hand and squeezed it.

"Unbelievably happy." She took a deep breath. Later, she'd cry for joy. Later, she'd tell him how impossible this all was. Later, she'd find a way to thank everyone who had allowed her to have this much happiness.

For now, she had to do her duty to her mother and her kin: introduce her new groom and his matriarch to her family, and make the formal announcement that made the marriage legally binding.

Today was good.

Tomorrow would be better.

As Grandmother made her way to greet the bridal party and Kamal stared in adoring devotion at his new bride, Kyvaan finally slipped away from the gathering. If he'd had to wait another minute knowing Dala was close he might have lost his composure.

Everyone from the bride's household was wearing the finest clothes heavily hung in jewels. Except one in plain, copper-colored silk.

The traditional punishment for an older sister who was censured before the Court of Matriarchs was to walk barefoot at her sister's wedding wearing only the plainest of clothes.

For years he'd been dueling with a Tanar-trained woman, the exiled older sister of his cousin's beloved, the promising student his grandmother had lost to a vicious attack. All the pieces of the puzzle fell into place. And, with her sister's marriage secure, Dala's exile was over.

A new chapter was starting.

Slipping between the shadows of the breezeway, he watched the night-flooded gardens until he saw the shimmer of silk between twining vines.

"It would be unwise to approach me unannounced in the dark," a familiar voice said. "The last man to do that earned a black eye, and left me a poor exile. I decided that if the situation occurred again, I'd leave a corpse by way of reproach."

Kyvaan stopped on the far side of the pillar, well out of reach of Dala, staring, the copper silk stunning against her dark skin, her eyes bright with mischief. "You're beautiful in the moonlight."

"And terrifying in the daylight?" There was a challenge in her voice, but a smile on her lips.

"Beautiful in the moonlight. Enchanting in daylight. The warm sun on a cold day. The bright moon on a dark night. The refreshing breeze in the midsummer desert."

"I thought you were a businessman, not a poet." She sat on the edge of the quiet fountain, black hair almost blue in the star-speckled darkness.

"I'm a man of Tanar. I can be both." He took a step forward.

Dala raised an eyebrow at the imposition. "Why are you here?"

"Three reasons. First, to thank you." He took another cautious step towards her.

A short laugh of surprise was quickly swallowed as she suppressed a smile. "For what did I earn this thanks?"

"For my cousin's happiness."

"I saw to my sister's happiness." She waved away his thanks. "Kamal is simply a lucky beneficiary of my sororal affection."

"I'll be sure to remind him of that when they have their first daughter." Another step.

"He granted my sister naming rights."

"I think your sister will be grateful too. Most those assets she listed were ones you had only a month ago." He was almost close enough to touch the trailing hem of her skirt.

Dala dipped her chin the way she did just before she metaphorically ripped out someone's jugular. "So your true reason for coming was to assess the competition?"

"Oh, no. I had you assessed many years ago. The second reason was to congratulate you."

"On the impending nuptial bliss of my sister?"

"On your well-won war with your enemies."

"What war?" Her posture was flawless as she held out an empty hand to the night air. "I don't see any blood."

Kyvaan stopped an arm's length away. "One of the first companies you bought with Dala Limited was Frontein. They were a small start-up that grew to challenge Lestrime Bloun Technologies, where House Ferith is heavily invested. You bankrupted Lestrime."

"I let them fail. There's a difference."

"House Ferith came to me for advice. Grandmother steered me away from them."

"As she should."

"And they went to Jonthir of House Thelwun to make a deal. Now House Thelwun is over-invested. They needed tonight's match to play out so they could have the respect of being tied to House Yalsmon. They failed. They'll be bankrupt within a month. The Council of Matriarchs will likely dissolve both houses by the end of the year and make the surviving daughters restart. The sons will be useless, unmarriable."

Dala shrugged. "And? Their choices are their own. House Ferith was teetering before Esko assaulted me. I was at least the second woman he attacked. The third was a married woman who works for the High Matriarch's guard. He mistook her for her younger sister. He's been in a desert exile for years, and the fall of his family's fortunes means he will never be redeemed.

"House Thelwun made a poor choice of allies and enemies. Had Jonthir properly courted Zuli, perhaps things would have gone differently. But—" Dala held her hands palm up in surrender. "I cannot control a man's choices. Only my own."

"Hmm." Kyvaan took the risk of sitting beside Dala.

Her smile turned sharp but her eyes sparkled in challenge. "Yes? You're confused about something?"

"Your mentor was the High Matriarch. Why didn't you go to her for help?"

Dala laughed.

It was a beautiful sound he wanted to drink in for the rest of his life.

Shaking her head, Dala said, "I spoke with her before my exile. She was my mentor when all was said and done, it is true. She offered to step in and save me. But why waste a favor on something I could do myself?"

"So you saved it to ensure my cousin arrived at your little sister's bridal night?"

Dala scoffed. "Oh, now I might have to think less of you. Why would I barter away a favor for something when I could make a deal? It is well known the High Matriarch cares dearly for her grandchildren. I had the name of the woman who made Kamal, the only living child of her eldest daughter, happy. That name alone was worth a fortune. An invite to the woman's bridal night was worth worlds."

Oh. That was highly specific. "Which worlds?"

"She gave me land rights on two of the moons in the outer system for the invite." Dala's smile turned smug. "And out-of-system trade rights for my family."

"I didn't hear your sister list them as part of her assets." They were nearly shoulder to shoulder.

Dala leaned towards him. "My sister is not my mother's only daughter who needs to be married," she whispered. "Zuli is married. My exile is over. She will move to her husband's house to inherit. I will inherit the Yalsmon fortune from my mother."

His eyes only dipped to her lips for a moment before he smirked. "That, Dala dearest, is the third reason I'm here."

"Oh? What is that?" She swept away from him again, leaving him space to retreat. "You've thanked me and congratulated me, what else is left to do? Perhaps you want to negotiate?"

"The third reason for chasing you into the dark garden, and the most important, is to ask when your bridal night will be. As you say, your mother has another daughter in need of a match."

She wrinkled her nose. "I do not know if I wish for a formal bridal night. My businesses are diverse, and I find I enjoy traveling off planet. My future husband, should I have one, would need to accept that."

Kyvaan leaned closer. "You will not be surprised to learn that I enjoy frequent travel."

"Yes, but you also have a family with political ties. There are expectations." Dala sighed and looked up at the stars.

"Kamal's mother was the Matriarch's heir. Still, it is possible we could be swept into the morass of Taran politics, but, would that be so awful? Aren't there things you'd want to change, if you were given the chance?"

"Are there things you'd change?" Dala countered.

He nodded. "Open the ports. Make the schools free. Balance the legal system so no more daughters of poor families are exiled for what the sons of the rich do."

That won him a smile. "Clever. You're good with words."

"I try to be."

"And you think you can win my heart? What makes you think I'd allow that?"

"You poured me a glass of wine. Doesn't dinner come next?"

She pursed her lips and surveyed him, leaning back with her eyes twinkling. "We can negotiate. After all, everything has a price."

ABOUT THE AUTHOR

IF YOU ASK, LIANA BROOKS WILL TELL YOU SHE HAS A VERY ordinary life. Her daily routines include driving kids to school, cooking meals, writing books, and reading. Truly, all very ordinary things.

If you ask about the scars on her hands, Liana will happily tell you about the moray eel named Baby who bit her while she was handing feeding it for a lab experiment, or about the bite marks from a small shark while she was diving off the coast of California, or a very vicious basketball game. Those stories are all true too.

If you ask where she lives, Liana might say Florida, Alaska, California, South Carolina, or Seoul in the Republic of Korea (South Korea, for the Americans). And she has lived in all those places.

If you ask her about her books, she'll tell you they're all wonderful. And they are! The *Fleet of Malik* books are perfect for readers who want a series of connected sci-fi romances about rebuilding after a decades long war. If it's the enemies-to-lovers trope you're after, try the super-hero series *Heroes and Villains*. The *Time and Shadows* time travel murder mysteries are wonderful for anyone more interested in a body count and crime than romance. And the *All I Want For Christmas* series is an escape into holiday romances that don't involve loving Christmases, moving to a small town, or giving up on your dreams.

You can find out more about Liana at her website, www.lianabrooks.com.

CHANGE OF MOMENTUM: *CHAPTER ONE*

THE HYPERTRAM FROM RYUN TO KYTAN WAS RUNNING THREE minutes late, a silver-blue moonbeam racing across the golden desert. It was one of the little inefficiencies that made Malcolm Long hate ground travel. That and the other passengers, of course.

Waving off an offer of food from the refreshment cart, he settled into a seat on the port side of the tram and bullishly stared out the window as they rushed across the barren rock between the city-states.

High overhead, a shining Koenig-1-11 caught the sunlight as it turned for a landing in Dreyun to the north.

Long's lips twitched into a frown as he pulled out his ever-present palm pad to take notes. The one-elevens were supposed to be phased out by now. Blue Sky Air Transport had been sold off six weeks ago to Lethe, and Lethe was replacing the one-elevens with the Koenig-360, a plane with a fabulous interior and fuel consumption that made him wince.

He assumed that was why Lethe had contacted his offices two days ago to request this meeting. They were paying for his travel, and had offered a consulting fee that was generous without being obscene.

The whole set-up made the hair on the back of his neck stand up.

Senior engineers at small research firms did not generally get attention like this. Especially since he hadn't published anything in over a year. His team had been busy, and he'd been juggling too many projects to finish anything of substance.

If this was about the Koenig-360s, he could handle the matter in a couple of weeks. If it wasn't...

An old fear clawed up his throat.

For a moment the crowded tram was silent, devoid of oxygen, cold as the dark between stars. Memories of pain and rage threatened to destroy him. His heart raced as he fought the fear. Pulled it under. Drowned it in the memories of today.

That had been another life.

Another name.

A time of power and cruelty—because the two always went hand in hand. But it was the past. He'd left the islands and there was no way Lethe could know who he had been.

Lips twitching into a grim smile, he checked his watch as the rocks gave way to the cultivated terraces of Kytan. Red rock formations ringed what were laughably called terraformed plateaus, bordered first with grain crops dividing the desert from the cultivated countryside, and then the land rippled inward past pools of pale pink water lilies, and into a sea of blue-green iridescent irises that sparkled like a dragonfly's wing.

Kytan was famous for the blooms that appeared for six weeks during the height of the Descent wedding season. Right now, the city-state was overflowing with tourists who wanted to wander the parks and young couples taking engagement photos for next summer.

The tram went straight to the hanging gardens hiding the terraced buildings at the heart of the city. The air was cooler there under the shade of the vines, effervescent with the scent of falling water, and the crowd hurried past him to catch the city transports while he walked, briefcase in hand, along a stream-lined road.

The artisinal waterway was filled with silvery-blue fish that swam through the sun-dappled water against the current flowing down from the step pyramids at the city center.

The original home of the Imperial Governor of Malik IV, designed to match the legendary summer palace of Emperor Insei Qui the Third, the pyramids in the center of the city were an architectural wonder, covered in towering waterfalls and fronds and vines of greenery. Great stone mountains built in the desert plain and covered with a deep green jungle, with flowers of brilliant white and pink burning along the branches like captured stars. The whole city sparkled like the dead emperor's scepter, exactly as the first arrivals from the old Empire had hoped.

"A thousand years of freedom and still we bow," Long murmured to himself. He couldn't remember the rest of the poem now, but he remembered when he'd first heard it, in the halls at school spoken by a girl who'd both captivated and challenged him.

She would have appreciated the architecture of Kytan. Probably had the opportunity to, considering her family and wealth.

Or perhaps not.

With the powerful families on the first continent, it all depended on who you knew and who you were allied with.

The Longs were a small family with no allies, unless his mother's book club friends counted, which he personally didn't feel they needed to. A family name, the right genes, a pittance of an inheritance, and an acre of land somewhere out in the wilds between city-states. It had been enough to get his family off the islands along the edge of the second continent and earn him a scholarship to the most prestigious university, but it wouldn't keep him alive if the Lethes wanted him dead.

Especially not here in their capital city.

"I suppose I should have asked for a bodyguard," he muttered to himself. One of the lab interns had the height and reach to be a good shield—but also the personality of a frightened rabbit, which might have made the graceless man more a liability than an asset.

Long followed the streams to the step pyramid and walked up the wide steps until he reached the main entrance. The arched glass doors opened into a chilled atrium, where the light passing through the waterfalls outside rippled and splashed over the dark marble floor.

Jewel-colored hummingbirds zipped past, chasing each other to the background music of a drowsy orchestral melody.

He felt he should applaud the theatrics, but restrained himself instead to a small half-smile.

The Lethes didn't sound like the kind of people who would enjoy his sense of humor.

A man in the Lethe colors of deep purple and slate gray approached him, white hair slicked back to an opalescent sheen. "May I help you, sir?"

"Doctor Malcolm Long. I have an appointment."

"Certainly, sir. If you'll please follow me."

He gestured to a bank of black lifts behind a discreet marble reception desk. The greeter stepped around and peered at a screen that Long had the good manners not to peek at.

Or at least not to get *caught* peeking at.

"You're a few minutes early, sir," the greeter said, glancing up at him with a moue of censure.

"My apologies. I have the day free if you would like me to wait." He must have rushed. *And now I look too eager*, he berated himself. On time was on time. Eager looked weak. Late was disrespectful. It was these little social mores that kept the culture of Descent afloat.

The greeter shook his head. "No, I apologize, sir. The computer recalculated the time based on the tram delay.

You have arrived on schedule, but a few minutes later would have been acceptable as well. If you'll take lift number seven, sir, it will take you to your meeting room."

That wasn't much information to go on.

Today's invitation had come from Lethe Corp, but without a signature. It was one of the annoying habits of the business people on the first continent that they used to keep their rivals guessing. Not knowing who he was meeting with meant he couldn't study or prepare for the meeting, not unless he wanted to study the several hundred middle managers, division leads, and board members.

He stepped into the mirrored elevator and tried to avoid glancing at his reflection, afraid he'd catch himself glaring and remember what a bad idea it was to get caught up in the machinations of political fanatics.

The mirror image glared back anyway.

For good reason, too; he should have worn a touch of Lethe purple somewhere to show a willingness to work together. The dark gray suit with a white shirt was a little too neutral. Long jerked the edge of one cuff straighter, an expression of annoyance tugging at his lips. He suppressed that too. This was a stupid risk to take. But declining, he suspected, would have proven fatal.

The door to the lift opened to a long, wide room with a row of slit windows overlooking the city. The only furniture was a white stone desk, carved to look like it had grown out of the stone floor. The walls were lined with silent waterfalls that pooled around the edge of the room, filled with small green reeds that had either been genetically engineered for the poor lighting or were fake; he couldn't tell at this distance.

At the desk, a woman was silhouetted by the window light, her pale hair swept up into a coiling, sleek up-do and held in place by a pin with a dripping chain of amethysts that matched her silk shirt. She was framed by the jungle outside, a pale diamond in the city of jewels. The effect was stunning, albeit contrived.

Long waited in front of the lift for her to acknowledge him as a dark suspicion formed.

Several minutes crept by before the woman finished her work, turned off her screen and stood. Recessed lights in the ceiling turned on as she moved, spotlighting Sonya Lethe, the sole heir of the Lethe fortune.

Fear crawled down his spine with cold fingers.

This is what a fish feels like when it sees a shark. I always wondered.

"Doctor Long, please, come in," she said from behind the desk. "I'm delighted you could make time in your schedule to come to Kytan today."

"The delight is mine," he said, repeating the proper polite phrasing. "I've been looking for an excuse to come to Kytan."

"Wedding season," Sonya said with a slink of a smile. "Is there someone you were hoping to show the flowers to?"

"Much to my mother's dismay, there is not."

Sonya walked around her desk and perched on the front edge. "Yes, she is Nettie Amherst of the Northland Amhersts, isn't she?"

"The last of that line to bear the Amherst name, yes." Sonya had done her homework, both a threat and a show of strength. Or maybe she thought it put them on equal footing. After all, any schoolchild raised on Descent could name the Lethe heirs back to the first ship.

"Perhaps your future spouse will see fit to revive the name. Long is...." She pursed her lips as she looked him up and down in an appraising way. "...Perhaps a little generic?"

He let the insult pass with a smile. "My father says it's a dialect word from the Grizhjan System meaning 'dragon'. I make it a rule never to argue translations with a linguist."

Sonya laughed. It was a calculated move, the arch of her neck, the degree of her smile, the uplift of her breasts, all mathematically designed to hide the fact that the muscles around her eyes never moved. She wasn't amused, she was manipulating him.

There were few things in the world that felt worse.

Long waited her out. Social graces did not require him to laugh along with her, so he didn't.

"Doctor Long, you look so grim. I do not like grim faces at business."

"Forgive me, Miss Lethe, I wasn't sure what response you anticipated. My name is not often a topic of conversation."

She smiled with an apologetic head tilt. "Engineers. You're always so delightfully focused, aren't you?"

"It's been mentioned before."

"Excellent." Sonya nodded. "Focus, I believe, is something this project needs. Please, take a seat." She brushed her hand along a control set in the stone desk and a chair materialized to one side, perfectly set to give the occupant a view of both the city and Sonya at their best angles.

Long regarded the chair with quiet suspicion. It was a trap, that much was obvious, but he wasn't sure exactly what kind.

Days like this, he thought about throwing it all away and moving back to the islands.

But then he'd never be able to fly again. And flying again was the only reason he kept breathing. Everything else was lost to him, but maybe, one day, he could reclaim the sky.

"It's quite safe," Sonya assured him as she took her own seat behind the desk. "The matter transporter is something new our research and development team is working on. It could replace all travel one day."

All the more reason to hate it.

Aloud he said, "I'd heard of research along those lines, but I thought we were decades away from a break-through." Unless someone was getting tech from the space fleet that had landed on the third continent. He, like most people, wasn't privy to the fine details of the treaty the planetary representative had signed with them, but he felt certain the tech they'd brought with them was off limits.

"This can only move objects a few feet. But it is fun to bring a chair in from the closet at the touch of a button. There's an awe factor I appreciate." She sat back with a smug smile, the empress on her throne.

"I can imagine." He took a seat and dutifully surveyed the view of the city.

Sonya sat in the chair across from him, blonde hair framed by the shimmering blue flowers. "Tell me, Doctor Long, do you have your father's gift for languages?"

The question blindsided him and he let a frown slip. "No. Some, I suppose. I speak all the regional cants of the first and second continents and can read the Journals Of Discovery in the original Imperial Script, but that's a talent any well-educated person on Descent can boast of." Especially since the dialects only changed a handful of slang terms between all of them. Calling them languages was a bit of an insult to the idea of diversity, really.

"You claim to have no gift for languages, but you broke the hardest cipher we know while at university." She laughed. "What a shame everyone isn't as lacking in gifts."

"Ah," he said, shrugging one shoulder in dismissal. "Cryptography is a ghost from my misguided youth." And he hadn't broken the cipher alone. The key to the whole thing had been in an obscure text his classmate had found.

Technically, he should have credited her, but that would have required finding her after the move to Descent, and he hadn't had the resources. And she was unlikely to want to speak to him ever again anyway.

"I work exclusively in aeronautical science now. That was why I thought you'd called me in, to solve the fuel efficiency problems with the Koenig-360?" He let the opening dangle.

Sonya waved the comment aside. "Planes are relics. We can burn all the fuel we want. In a few years the new matter transporters will be the foundation of Lethe's transportation division. Let the Koenigs fly. This project is much more time sensitive." She held up a datcube, black and small enough to be concealed in his fist.

Long raised an eyebrow in question.

"This belonged to one of my employees. At the time of his death he had no heir, so the data became company property."

How convenient for Lethe.

"My techs have been able to decrypt a portion of the data on here, but the rest is beyond them. We've applied to other experts Lethe already has a working relationship with, but neither were able to decrypt it. Both experts mentioned you." She held the datcube out to him.

It was heavier than its size suggested. Someone had coated it in the anti-theft paint that had been popular for the past two years—which meant it wasn't too old to be recoverable—but on one side he felt an indentation, as if someone had pierced the cover with a fingernail.

It was all too easy to picture the previous owner holding this in a death grip in their final moments.

A sense of inevitable dread settled over him. It had been a mistake accepting the Lethe's offer. A mistake to be found on their radar at all. If he couldn't untangle him-self—quickly—he would undoubtedly meet the same fate as the datcube's luckless owner.

"Have you considered the possibility that the infor-mation is corrupted?" Long asked. "I can guess which experts you would speak to, and who would recommend me, and there's very little I could do that they wouldn't have. There's no point in wasting your time if the data isn't salvageable."

Sonya shrugged. "I give it a twelve percent chance of being corrupted. It might be a keyed cypher, but the balance of probability says it's most likely an encryption."

"And the data?"

"Time sensitive only because of the employee's death."

A thin thread of hope appeared. "I realize it's tactless to ask, but is this datcube part of an ongoing investigation into that death? My clearance for several of my projects requires me to steer clear of the Jhandarmi and all local constabulary." *Please say yes.*

Sonya gave him another calculated smile, this one undoubtedly meant to make her look innocent and charming. "The employee died because of a burst heart. The coroner ruled it death of natural causes."

The coroners of Descent would rule a stab wound death by natural causes if the right people asked. It was a line of thought he didn't dare to follow. "The best I can offer is to look at the encryption. Without seeing it I can't tell you anything more."

"Can you have a status report to me by the end of the week?" Sonya asked with a polite smile that said 'No' wasn't an acceptable answer.

Three days to unlock the datcube and analyze the contents was a tight timeline if he wanted to focus on his other work, but it was doable. He nodded. "A status report, but nothing more. Do you have a copy of the cube that I can take with me?"

Her lips slipped into an uncharacteristic grimace. "That is our only copy."

"Ah." He set it down on the desk between them. "That makes security problematic."

"Your lab is secure?" she asked.

"The research lab is, but the outer office is designed with client comfort in mind."

Sonya nodded in understanding. "The datcube will be sent by armed courier. Lethe can offer you the standard security fee for priority technology as well as a consultant fee." She twisted the screen on her desk he could see the numbers.

Standard fees, nothing that raised any red flags, although the whole affair seemed suspect.

"If you are able to decode the data, there will be a sizable bonus. Have you ever worked with Lethe before?"

"I've never had the pleasure." Just as he'd never had the pleasure of being burned alive before. It was one of those little life-threatening things he'd made sure to avoid.

She pulled a paper contract from her desk drawer. "This is our consulting contract. While working on this project, you are not considered a Lethe employee and will not receive shares, benefits, or protections from Lethe. You will be paid commensurate to your skill level, and at the rate agreed. The contract terminates automatically after six weeks, unless both parties agree to extend the contract. Before, during, and after this project you are forbidden from disclosing the focus of the project with anyone other than your Lethe contact. Do you have any questions?"

Long looked over the paperwork. "Do you have the work of the previous groups that tried to decrypt this cube?"

"Would it be useful?" Sonya tilted her head.

"Knowing what they tried and what failed will save me time." And it would tell him who she had trusted.

Another small frown. "The other experts said they didn't want to be influenced by other people's processes." There was a hit of censure in her tone.

"We all approach work differently," he said. "I will probably look at it before reviewing their notes, but I don't feel the need to reinvent the wheel. Appearing like a genius to the world usually involves standing on the backs of geniuses who came before. It's how I did the decryption that I published in university."

Sonya gave a small nod, but he could see that she'd deducted a few points from the imaginary tally. "In that case, I'll make their work available to you. The records and a machine to process it on will arrive tomorrow. It goes without saying that everything stored on the computer becomes the property of Lethe after the contract is over."

"Of course." He made a mental note to scrub the machine for spyware and keep it away from his work lab and notes when it arrived. Lethe hadn't made their empire by playing fair.

Sonya stood up. "Then all is in order."

Following her lead, he stood too.

She posed, probably trying to look seductive. "I look forward to working with you, Doctor Long."

"And I look forward to working with you." As much as he looked forward to being eaten alive by ant lions. It was a trap, and the only way to escape was to move forward. If he could get Sonya the information maybe—just maybe—he'd escape with his life.

Keep reading! Head to
www.inkprintpress.com/lianabrooks/
malik/change/
to buy your copy now!

BODIES IN MOTION
Fleet of Malik

A civil war tore them apart. Can a cold war bring them back together?

Available from all major retailers.
www.inkprintpress.com/lianabrooks/
malik/bodies/

LIANA BROOKS
EVEN VILLAINS FALL IN LOVE
HEROES AND VILLAINS